Phil Cummings was born ... the seaside town of Port Broughton on South Australia's Yorke Peninsula. The youngest of eight children, he was surrounded by storytellers and lived a life full of adventure!

After many years as a teacher of young children in Adelaide's northern suburbs, Phil now writes full time. He lives in the Adelaide foothills with his wife, two children, a dog, two chickens, a budgie, eight goldfish and several possums.

www.philcummings.com

Author's note

We lived in a very small country town until I was nine years old. The stories in this book are based loosely on those memories. My father died when I was eleven and my brother David – Sam in this book – died in 1974. I am delighted to include some of my treasured memories of them both in this book.

Danny Allen was here

PHIL CUMMINGS

ILLUSTRATED BY DAVID COX

PAN
Pan Macmillan Australia

First published 2007 in Pan by Pan Macmillan Australia Pty Limited
1 Market Street, Sydney

National Library of Australia
Cataloguing-in-Publication data:

Cummings, Phil, 1957– .
Danny Allen was here.

For ages 9 and over.

ISBN 978 0 330 42294 9.

I. Cox, David, 1933– . II. Title.

A823.3

Typeset in 12.5/16 pt Bembo by Midland Typesetters, Australia
Printed in Australia by McPherson's Printing Group

Papers used by Pan Macmillan Australia Pty Limited are natural, recyclable products
made from wood grown in sustainable forests. The manufacturing processes conform
to the environmental regulations of the country of origin.

*To my father, mother, brothers and sisters
with thanks for a wonderful childhood.*

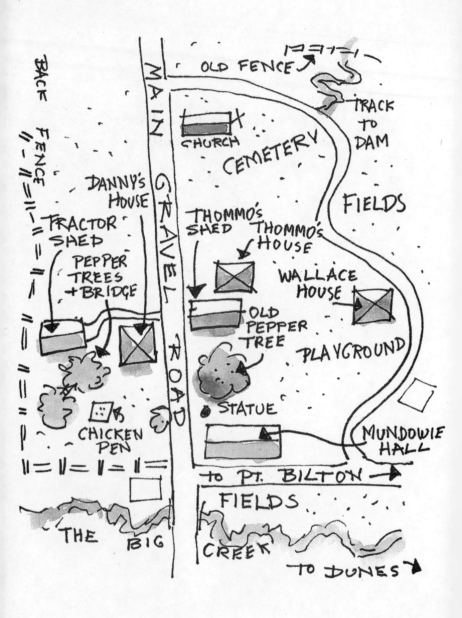

Contents

1
One Each

The morning sun peeked over the hills and shone down on the small town of Mundowie. Long shadows stretched across fields, dry creek beds and white gravel roads. Roosters that had never met crowed to each other across the little town. A flock of noisy white cockatoos took flight from the gums by the big creek and shredded the sky. They headed for Danny Allen's house. Out of the shadows of the creek, over the Mundowie Institute Hall and across the wide gravel road they flew.

The cockatoos were squawking overhead, their swift shadows scarring the ground, when Danny Allen and his small dog, Tippy, burst through the rickety old blue screen door – *bang!* – and onto the front verandah. Tippy ran down the steps (there were four of them), stopped at the bottom and stood wagging his tail, panting, looking back up at Danny, waiting, as if to say, *Come on, what are we doing? Where are we going? What's happening?*

Danny stood on the edge of the verandah, raised a hand to shield his squinting eyes and looked up at the cockatoos. He smiled down at Tippy then spread his arms like wings and leapt from the top step into the sunshine.

'Squaaaaawwk!' he cried. The cockatoos ignored him. Tippy danced excitedly and spun around on his hind legs like a dog in a faraway circus. *Yap! Yap!*

Danny raced out the rusty front gate that was never closed and onto the dusty footpath. Looking left then right he ran hard across the wide gravel road that cut through the middle of the town. Tippy was right beside him. Danny slapped his hip. 'Come on, boy, let's go. Come on.' Tippy was a terrier, his fur a jigsaw of black and white patches. His thin black tail was curly like a spiral and had a white tip.

Danny's boots were floppy (no socks, laces untied) and his shorts were twisted crookedly. Running wasn't easy. He'd dressed hurriedly in clothes he'd scooped up from the floor by his bed. The white T-shirt he was wearing belonged to his big brother, Sam, and flapped from his back like a torn sail.

Danny headed for his lookout tree across the road. It was a huge pepper tree that shaded the large white soldier statue in front of the Mundowie Institute Hall. The tree was old and the roots gripped the earth like an old man's fingers. There were lumps and bumps and twisted branches all the way up the trunk. To Danny, they were little steps perfect for climbing.

Danny stood under the tree and glanced up into the tangle of branches. Sunlight sparkled through the leaves. Danny squinted. Tippy trotted up to him and sat at his feet. He loved his days with Danny.

Danny squatted down. He took his small dog's head gently in his hands, rubbed his ears with twiddling thumbs and looked him in the eye. 'You wait here, Tippy boy,' he said. 'I'm going up to see what I can see.' Danny took a deep breath through his nose and rolled his eyes to the sky. 'This is going to be an amazing day, boy. I can smell it.' Danny started to climb.

Tippy sat and watched, tilting his head curiously from side to side. Danny was quick like a monkey. He could climb this tree faster than his brother, Sam, something of which he was very proud.

Danny pulled himself up onto his favourite branch.

It was thick and reminded him of an elephant's trunk. He was higher than the white soldier statue.

There was a thinner branch just above his head. When he stood he held it to balance himself. On days when the wind was wild and his branch swayed he would pretend he was surfing the sky.

Not today though, because there was no wind. The day was hot and humid. Like a pirate in a crow's nest Danny stood up and peered through the curtain of leaves in front of him. He could see the entire town. Mundowie was only a small place, with seven houses, a church, the cemetery and the Mundowie Institute Hall.

Danny looked straight across the road to his house. The tin roof was speckled with rust. His little sister, Vicki, appeared on the verandah and began spinning around a post near the front door. She started singing as if the verandah were a stage. As she spun, the dress she was wearing flared out like an umbrella. Danny looked to the back of the house.

The chickens were crowding near the tractor shed. Danny's mum was throwing them seed like a magician throws magic dust. Another two huge old pepper trees, just like the one he was standing in, stood beside the tractor shed like giant guards on sentry duty.

Danny turned to his right. He could see the church on the edge of town and his dad on a growling tractor bumping across the top of a hill beyond that.

Then Danny heard a distant rumble echo across the sky to his left. He looked down at Tippy. 'Did you hear that?' he called.

Tippy lifted one ear.

'That was thunder!' Danny cried. He sidled along his branch. He felt the breath of a breeze. 'I reckon it's going to rain! I told you this would be an amazing day.' Danny parted the thick leaves and peered out.

He looked left to the horizon beyond the big creek. There were thick clouds bulging like muscles. The clouds were dark and the colour of the bruise on Sam's leg where the cricket ball had hit him.

Danny took a deep breath. 'Smell the rain, Tippy. Can you smell it, boy? Can you smell the rain?'

Suddenly a small stone whizzed through the leaves behind him and just missed his head. Danny nearly lost his balance. 'Hey!'

'Danny! Get down here. Quick!'

Danny peered down to see his brother, Sam, standing under the tree.

Sam was tall and thin. He didn't have Danny's fat cheeks or chubby legs. And his hair, although straight like Danny's, was dark, almost black. Danny's hair was light brown. Sam had the same eyes as Danny though – deep brown. Chocolate drops, their mother called them.

'Don't throw stones!' Danny grumbled.

Sam looked around suspiciously. 'Just come down here,' he hissed.

'If you're going to tell me about the thunder,' said Danny, 'I heard it.'

'Don't worry about that,' said Sam, 'I've got something great to tell you.' Sam's voice was strangely quiet and he was looking around as if he were a spy in danger.

Danny squatted on his branch. He was suspicious. Sam often set traps for him. Like the time he waited in the bedroom in the dark and stuck a hairy monster mask over the light switch. He had even put grease on the eyeballs.

When Danny had fumbled in the dark for the switch and felt skin, hair and slimy eyeballs, he screamed the loudest he had ever screamed in his life. He wasn't going to fall victim to his brother's tricks again.

Danny pulled the branches apart and peered out across the town. He couldn't see anyone. 'Why are you whispering?' he asked.

'If you come down I'll tell you,' said Sam.

Danny hesitated. Sam moved closer to the trunk.

A breeze came and whispered through the leaves.

'Come on, hurry up. I want you to come with me,' Sam said.

'Where are you going?'

Sam craned his neck and narrowed his eyes. 'I'm

going on a . . .' he paused and thought carefully. 'On a . . . secret mission.'

Danny's ears pricked up when he heard the words *secret mission*. He liked the sound of that.

Sam suddenly changed his approach. He shrugged his shoulders. 'But that's okay,' he said as he turned casually away. 'If you don't want to come, then just forget it. I'll go by myself.'

Tippy sat up, his left ear bent as if broken, and looked from Danny to Sam then back to Danny again. He knew something was about to happen.

Sam started to walk slowly away.

'All right! Hold on!' Danny called. 'I'm coming down.'

Danny scrambled down and jumped to the ground – *thump*. He stood looking expectantly into Sam's eyes.

Sam frowned at Danny and tugged at his shirt.

'Hey! That's my shirt.'

'Forget that,' said Danny. 'What's the big secret? Where are we going?'

Sam smiled, his brilliant white teeth gleaming from his dusty face. He clasped Danny's shoulders. 'Remember the tadpoles Dad got for us last year?'

'Yeah.'

'Remember the pond we dug for them by the chicken yard and the island we made in the middle that looked like Tasmania?'

'Yeah.'

'And the frog racing after that?'

'Yeah, yeah.'

'Well, you know that rain we had the other week?'

'Yeah.'

'It was good, wasn't it?'

'Yeah, I thought it was, but Dad said it was useless. He said we needed it ages ago.'

'Yeah, but it *was* good for them.'

'Good for who?' Danny frowned.

Sam straightened himself. 'Well, guess what?'

Danny widened his eyes; the secret was coming. 'What?'

Sam raised his eyebrows. 'Mark Thompson told me that there are tadpoles at the dam. They're hidden in little pools in the reeds in the small creek there.'

Danny looked suddenly worried. It was now clear to him why this was a big secret. They had been told *never* to go near the dam alone. It was just outside the town, past the church and down a small dirt track. They had to crawl through a fence and walk over a hill.

He felt a shiver prickle his spine. Inside his head he heard the echo of his mother's voice. *Don't you* ever *go near the dam! The water is so cold and the sides so slippery you will fall in and never get out.*

He could feel her thin finger jabbing rhythmically at his chest emphasising each word. *Don't . . . ever . . .*

go . . . near . . . the . . . dam! And put your boots on when you go outside. There are snakes about.

Danny straightened his shorts. 'But you know what Mum says about the dam.'

Sam patted him on the shoulders. 'Duh! Mum's not going to know, is she? This is a *secret* mission, remember? We won't tell anyone!'

Danny hesitated. 'Maybe we should wait for Dad to take us; then we can all go like last time.'

'Dad hasn't got time. *We* have to go.' Sam tightened his grasp on Danny's shoulders and shook him gently. 'You do want tadpoles, don't you?'

There was only one answer to that question.

'Yeah.' Danny nodded.

'Right,' said Sam. 'Come on, then. We'll be frog racing in no time. I'm going to get the biggest tadpole I can find.'

◆

They marched across the road. Tippy followed. Sam had planned everything.

'We have to go home first,' he said.

Danny walked quickly to keep up. 'What for?'

'A big tin.'

Sam led Danny through the front gate. They hurried along the cracked path to the verandah. 'Stay low,' said Sam. 'Don't let Mum see you.'

Danny was excited. He felt like a real spy.

They crouched low and moved along the verandah to the side of the house. Tippy followed curiously. With their backs against the wall the boys looked down the long stony driveway to the shed.

Tippy looked as well.

Sam clutched Danny's arm. 'I'll keep watch. You go down and get the tin.'

Danny nodded.

Sam continued. 'There's a big one with a wire handle under the workbench near the vice, next to the old drawers with all the nuts and bolts in them.'

Sam twisted his head sharply this way and that. 'Ready?'

Danny nodded.

'Right, all clear.' He pushed Danny in the back. 'Go!'

Danny had no time to discuss the plan. He was off! The noise of his feet crunching on the stones of the driveway made him nervous. Crouching low, he waddled, duck-style, under the kitchen window. He rose slowly and took a peek at his mother.

She was cooking and covered in flour. The radio was on and she was wriggling her hips. Danny smiled. Her long hair was pushed into untidy bunches with brown clips and some wispy strands hung at her shoulders. The apron she was wearing was covered in wild flowers. It had one torn pocket and tattered lacy frills. A song she

liked came on the radio. She turned it up and began singing at the top of her voice. Danny couldn't stand her singing. He crept quickly on his way.

Finding the tin was easy. The spider webs hanging from the old wardrobe didn't worry Danny. He ducked under them, then looked into the shadows under the bench and spotted the tin. It was an old tin from the kitchen and Danny's dad had twisted wire to make the handle.

Danny snatched the tin and scampered out of the shed. On the way back up the driveway his foot kicked a pothole. He nearly fell and the tin rattled, but he made it back without being seen.

'Well done,' said Sam, patting him on the back.

Danny felt good. He puffed up proudly. 'It was easy,' he said.

Excited, they walked quickly out the driveway. Two chickens followed, but Tippy chased them flapping back into the yard.

The boys were at the edge of the road and about to cross when they were startled by the squeal of the front screen door being thrown open. They froze, thinking it was their mother, and they turned slowly, their wide dark eyes rolled toward the door. It wasn't their mother they saw on the verandah; it was their little sister, Vicki.

She danced up to a post, took hold of it and spun herself around. She was wearing the thin white dress their mum had made for her. It was her favourite. She liked the way it fanned out from her knees when she twirled.

Spinning once around the post, she jumped from the verandah and skipped happily toward her brothers. Her long hair flapped across her shoulders.

Vicki squinted up at the sky. 'I heard the thunder, boys, did you?' she said. Vicki spied the big tin behind Sam's back. 'Hey, what's that for?' she asked, craning her neck to see. 'Have you got something in there? Show me.'

Sam tipped the tin upside down. 'No, nothing.'

'What's it for, then?'

Sam and Danny exchanged shifty glances.

'Nothing,' they chorused.

Vicki put her hands on her hips. 'I know when you're lying.' Pointing a sharp finger and frowning, she said, 'You can't keep secrets and tease me, remember? Mum said!'

'There's no secret,' said Sam. 'Honest.'

Vicki had him cornered and she knew it. 'If there's no secret then I'm going to come and see what you put in the tin.' She smiled and wriggled her hips to make her dress twirl.

'You can't come,' said Danny sharply. 'We're going to the dam to get tadpoles.'

Sam nudged him with his elbow. 'Danny! What did you tell her that for?'

'It just came out.'

Vicki's face lit up. 'I want to come! Can I? Can I?'

Sam shook his head. 'No, you can't.'

Vicki looked at Sam smugly. She folded her arms. 'Then I'll tell Mum.'

There was silence. Sam flipped his cap off, ruffled his hair, sighed, and then put it back on again. 'Okay then, we'll be quick,' he said as he moved to look Vicki in the eye. He clasped her shoulders just as he had done with Danny under the pepper tree. 'Now listen, you have to do what I say though, *exactly* what I say.'

Vicki smiled and nodded. 'I will, I will do what you say,' she said.

'You'd better,' Sam warned.

◆

Vicki was happy. It showed in the way she skipped and danced across the road. She chatted and sang all the way.

Tippy was happy as well. His tail didn't stop wagging and he sniffed every post he passed. They walked past the church and out of the town.

A tall forest of wild yellow weeds lined the dirt track to the dam. The fence they had to climb through was made of barbed wire and was old and rusty with rotten posts. Some had fallen and were half-buried in small dunes of red sand.

Danny held the wire up for Vicki, but she still managed to tear her dress a little. She sat in the sand and looked at the hole. Her finger poked through. 'You did that, Danny!' she said crossly.

Danny decided to distract her. 'Quick! Get up!' he cried. 'There are ants down there.'

Vicki jumped to her feet and snatched at Danny's shirt-tails, brushing her behind madly. 'I don't like ants.' The hole in her dress was forgotten.

Sam led them quickly up the slope that was the

bank of the dam. Danny felt like an explorer as they reached the top and looked out over the water. There wasn't a ripple. The water was like a giant mirror; he could see the reflection of the darkening sky.

To their left was the small creek that flowed into the dam when the rain came. The last time Danny had stood in its dry bed the creek's sides only came up to his head. It was narrow and cut a twisted course down a gentle slope to the dam. A few scratchy bushes lined its banks. The thick forest of reeds at the mouth of the creek was where pools formed. Sam suddenly grabbed Danny's arm and pointed to them. He spied sunlight glinting off water. 'That's where the tadpoles will be!' he cried. 'Let's go!'

Down the slope they ran. Sam led the way, his arms flailing, trying to keep balance. 'Whoa! I'm going to fall!' he laughed.

Danny was right behind him. 'Look out! I'm coming through.'

Vicki couldn't keep up. 'Wait for me! Waaaiiiit!'

Tippy left them and went to the edge of the dam to drink.

They reached the reeds and ran up and down the bank of the dam searching for the best spots. From where Danny was standing it looked like a miniature canyon.

Vicki slipped and trod in mud. Some splattered onto her dress. 'Yuck!'

Sam knelt at the side of a weedy pool. He put the tin by his side. Beneath his wide-eyed reflection he spied movement. He pushed his giant hand into the watery world and began hunting. 'There are heaps in here!' he said.

Danny crouched beside him. The small pool of water was wild with tadpoles. Danny couldn't believe his eyes. 'Look at them!'

'Don't just look at them, catch them!' said Sam.

There was splashing, laughing and shrill cries of delight. Sam scooped up water with his hands. He was a good tadpole catcher.

Danny caught a couple, but Vicki only caught blobs

of mud so she gave up. She squatted by the tin and guarded the writhing prisoners. She stuck her hands in and let the tadpoles tickle her palms. Before long the tin was nearly full of water. When Danny looked in and saw the frenzy of trapped tadpoles stirring the water he thought they must have at least a million! But that was just a rough guess.

The hunt was suddenly interrupted by a tremendous *crack* of thunder. Everyone jumped. They all stopped and lifted their heads. The sky had darkened suddenly. Wind pushed into their backs. The reeds swayed and crackled, then a flash of brilliant lightning forked in jagged streaks across the sky.

Crack! Vicki cringed as the thunder rumbled away in booming echoes. She walked over to stand with Sam. 'I want to go home,' she whimpered.

'Hang on,' said Sam. 'I'll just get a couple more.'

He stared at the water: hovering, waiting, hunting.

Vicki hung on to his shoulder, her eyes rolling to the sky. Beyond the reflection of his little sister's worried face Sam could see the tadpoles dodging and weaving through reed stalks and green slime. He placed his hands in the water and waited for a tadpole to swim into his trap. He was about to pounce when a huge drop of rain fell into the water and distracted him. *Ploop.*

More fat raindrops fell, splashing cool on Sam's

back. His reflection crinkled as the pool of water he was peering into was rippled with rings.

Danny had moved to stand halfway up the bank. He watched as the first drops bombed the dam and a million circles appeared. The splash of cool water on his neck and shoulders made him giggle.

He spread his arms like wings and watched the huge droplets explode on his skin. Then he tilted his head back and looked up. Lines of rain came spearing down at him. Heavy droplets, cool and fresh, landed in his eyes. So he closed them and felt the weight of the rain on his eyelids. Cool water splashed on his cheeks. The best feeling was when he stuck his tongue out and tasted the rain.

Then, another rumble of thunder, louder than the first, saw the rain come pounding down, drumming loud and hard. Tippy barked at the sky as little rivers began running around Danny's feet.

'Okay!' Sam said. 'Let's go!'

Danny looked at the creek.

Through a curtain of wild rain and beads of water hanging from his furrowed brow, Danny saw Vicki reach for the tin. 'I'll save the tadpoles,' she cried. With two hands wrapped around the wire handle Vicki bent her knees slightly to lift the tin. She wobbled and teetered, then skidded and slipped. She was like a newborn lamb trying to stand.

Sam moved to help. 'Put the tin down!' he called. 'It's too heavy for you! You're going to dr . . .'

Too late. Down she tumbled. The tin fell from her hands and rolled bumping and rattling down the bank toward the dam. The water flowed from the tin in a flood and emptied the tadpoles into the dam.

The tadpoles were gone and Sam was furious.

Vicki squinted through the rain and sat in the mud sad and silent.

Sam ground his teeth angrily. 'You just don't listen, do you?' he yelled as he marched to stand over Vicki. 'I told you to leave it! I said when we came that you had to do what I said!'

Sam turned his back and climbed up the bank. 'You can get the tin. *I'm* not!' He marched up and hit Danny on the arm as he passed. 'Let's go!'

Danny looked back at Vicki. She was wet and muddy and her hair hung like cooked spaghetti. The tin was lying at the edge of the water.

'Bring the tin,' said Danny, turning his back on her. 'We have to go home.' He trotted off to catch Sam.

Along the track the boys ran, bombing big puddles with their pounding feet. They laughed. Tippy dodged their explosions.

They ran across the road, down the driveway and into the back shed. The sound of the rain on the tin roof was loud as they shook themselves like dogs. The doors were open and water streamed over the gutter. Danny felt as though he were behind a waterfall in a cave.

With flat hands Sam suddenly chopped at the waterfall and splashed Danny. 'Ha, ha, ha. I got you in the face!' he said.

Danny retaliated, but Sam jumped back. 'Ha, ha, you missed, Danny! You missed!' The game was on.

Tippy barked at the frenzy of the water war. The boys laughed hard and played wildly. In some places the water made thin panes like glass. The boys loved shattering them.

The rain was easing when they heard their mother open the back door. 'Children, come inside and dry yourselves,' she called. 'Hurry up.'

Pushing and bumping, dripping and skidding, the boys stumbled into the kitchen. It was warm and smelt of biscuits.

Tippy shook himself and so did the boys. They were giggling.

Their mother turned and smiled. Specks of flour dotted her cheeks. With a funny puff from her bottom lip she tried to blow an annoying strand of hair from her eyes. 'Haven't I told you not to stay out in the open when there's lightning about?' She paused and looked toward the back door. 'And where's Vicki?' she asked, matter-of-factly.

Danny stopped giggling.

Drips fell from his nose. His breathing quickened. His eyelashes fluttered wildly and his heart pounded up to his throat.

Vicki!

He looked sharply at Sam.

The dam!

He could feel his mother staring at him. 'Was Vicki out there with you?' she asked.

Silence. Danny's eyes darted to Sam then back to his mother. Suddenly Danny felt icy cold and began to shake. He felt his jaw drop as his mother looked into his shifting eyes. It was as if she could see behind them into Danny's mind. Her happy face changed, just like the sky at the dam, to dark and gloomy.

She knew there was something wrong. She turned to Sam and frantically wiped her hands with her apron.

'Where is she, Sam?'

Danny's eyes were bulging when he looked to his older brother. *Please tell her*, he thought, *please. The dam! The water is so cold and the sides so slippery.*

Sam took short sharp breaths. His nose was twitching and his dark eyebrows folded and unfolded. 'I'm . . . I'm sorry, Mum, we . . . we didn't . . .'

His mother shook him. She didn't mean to do it hard but she did. 'Where is Vicki?' she cried.

Sam looked as though he might be sick when he finally said, 'We left her at the dam, Mum.'

The kitchen wasn't warm any more and the boys stood like statues as their mother flung her apron onto the mountain of delicately balanced dishes on the sink.

Into the throat of the passage she ran, her desperate feet thumping the floorboards. The boys followed. There was a loud creaking thud as the front door was thrown open.

From the verandah they leapt wildly into the rain and Danny saw his mum kick off her shoes as they crossed the road. They were her best shoes – the shiny black ones with the ribbons at the front.

Running barefoot in mud was usually good fun, but this time it wasn't. His mother was swift. Danny pumped his arms and legs as fast as they would go. *I'm sorry, Vicki! I'm sorry, Vicki!* he kept saying inside his head.

Along the track they ran. They scrambled through the tangle of the old fence.

Danny slipped and struggled up the hill. He was the last one to run up the bank of the dam. With every step he took all he could think of was that he was going to see his little sister floating on top of the water like an angel flying.

He stood at the top of the bank, puffing hard and searching desperately. The dam was riddled with never-ending circles. Danny swallowed. The tadpole tin had gone and so had Vicki.

Sam was standing, saying nothing, just staring at the water. Danny looked at his mother running along the edge of the dam, searching and yelling.

'Vicki! Vicki!'

Her head was flicking back and forth, back and forth.

'Vicki! Vickiiiiii!'

Danny wanted to call but couldn't find his voice. If only he could call her name she might hear him. She might come and be all right. Inside his head his voice was loud, screeching. *Vicki! Vicki!* But he couldn't say it out loud. He tried and he tried. His jaw quivered, he made soft squealing noises, but he had no voice.

He felt hot and sweaty then cold and shivery. A pain came to his chest. He found it hard to breathe. The louder his mother screamed the more Danny felt like crying. Images of Vicki spinning around the verandah post flashed rapidly in front of him. Time and time again they danced behind his eyes like instant replays. All he wanted was to see Vicki. All he wanted was to hear her annoying singing. All he wanted was to say sorry.

The world suddenly changed as the clouds began to break apart. The rain eased and Danny shivered all over.

Still his mother screamed. Light came peeking through and sunbeams spot lit the world. Danny looked across the dam through glistening threads of silver rain. He hung his head, then licked his lips and tasted the salt of tears.

Sam suddenly hollered, '*Mum! Look!*'

Danny spun to see Sam pointing toward the reeds of the small creek.

Tippy was at the reeds before any of them. He was jumping and bounding, his tail spinning like a helicopter blade. He danced on his hind legs and the reeds moved.

A hand appeared and pulled the reeds apart. Vicki pushed her face through the reeds as if peeking out from behind a curtain. Then up out of the creek she scrambled, covered in mud from head to toe.

Vicki's white dress was clinging to her skin and thick mud gelled her hair into rat-tail strands. She was very surprised to see everyone there to meet her, especially her mum.

Her muddy face lit up and her white teeth shone brilliantly. 'Hey Mum!' She grinned cheerily. 'Hey boys!'

Their mother ran, fell to her knees and cuddled Vicki, but Vicki pushed her away. 'Don't, Mum,' she frowned. 'You'll spill them again!'

Her mother sniffed away tears. 'Spill what?'

'The surprise,' Vicki smiled proudly.

The mud all over Vicki's face made her blue eyes sparkle more than ever before.

'Tah dah!' she cried, as she pulled the big tin from the reeds and walked toward her brothers.

'Look in there, boys,' she said as she placed the tin carefully in front of Danny and Sam. 'Go on. Look.' She wanted to twirl, but the mud was slippery and she didn't want to fall into the dam – *the sides so slippery and the water so cold*. And anyway, her dress wouldn't fan out, it was too heavy with mud.

The boys peered into the tin. There was a shallow pool of murky water. Swimming about happily in the water were three tadpoles.

'I couldn't get any more,' said Vicki. 'They were all too slimy.'

She pushed her muddy face between the shoulders of her two brothers. 'But that's enough, 'cause it means we can have one each.'

Their mother took hold of Vicki's hand. 'Thank goodness you're okay,' she said.

'Yep,' said Vicki. 'I'm fine.' Then she looked up at her mum. 'Are you okay, Mum?'

Their mother nodded.

Everything was quiet for a while. Then Danny pointed and said, 'Can I have that fat one?'

Vicki shook her head. 'No, that's mine! I got 'em so I get to choose.'

Sam glanced down at Vicki's thin muddy legs. He saw blood.

'Your knee is bleeding,' he said.

Vicki looked at the small trickle of blood. She hadn't noticed it until Sam pointed it out. Her face suddenly buckled. 'It really hurts,' she whined.

Their mother knelt to look. 'Don't worry about that,' she said, dabbing gently at the blood with a wet handkerchief. 'I'll fix it when we get home.'

'You let Danny carry the tin and I'll give you a piggyback,' said Sam.

'Will you carry me *all* the way home?'

Sam nodded. 'Hmm, yeah, all right, all the way. I might have to stop for a rest though.'

Sam dropped to his knees and Vicki climbed onto his back. The rain stopped as quickly as it had started.

And so off they went, Danny with the treasure in the tin, Tippy at his heels as usual, Sam with a wild rider whipping his back and their mother trailing close behind. She would wait to get them safely home before she gave them the growling talk. They strode back along the track and past the church.

When the cockatoos flew squawking from the gum trees near the Mundowie Institute Hall they circled overhead and Vicki tossed her head back, laughing and squawking just like them.

Danny looked up to the cockatoos and then to the clouds beyond. They were breaking up and floating in dark islands across an ocean of blue sky.

The sun came out. Beads of water had collected on the rusty barbed-wire fences. Danny looked at his pepper tree as he crossed the road and headed for home. The world around was sparkling, like it always did after rain. Then, *crack*!

The thunder made them jump.

'Run Sam! Run!' Vicki cried, hitting her brother hard.

'You just hang on,' said Sam, galloping along. 'If you fall off it will hurt!'

'I know that,' Vicki replied.

She turned to Danny. 'Don't drop the tadpoles, Danny! Or else!'

Danny stuck his tongue out at his sister. When she had turned away and yelled at Sam again, Danny slowed his run and peered into the tin. The tadpoles looked happy.

Danny felt happy too. 'One, two, three,' he counted. 'Yep, that's one each.'

Then he lifted his eyes to the sound of his mother's voice.

'Slow down please, Sam,' she called as she picked up her shoes from the side of the road.

'No, don't,' Vicki laughed. 'Faster! Faster!'

Danny smiled.

2
Surfing the Dune

The big creek was a wild place.

'Come on, Danny!' Sam called, his voice echoing around the treetops. 'Hurry up if you're coming!' Sam was running along the edge of the big creek where the red-earth cliffs were highest. Danny was trying to keep up but he didn't want to fall; it was a long way down to the rocky creek bed. Danny guessed it would be further than falling from the roof of the house. He'd been up on the roof to get a ball the day before and ended up sitting on the very top, near the chimney, to watch the sunset. Yesterday's sunset seemed such a long time ago.

Danny bounded determinedly through the tall grass, dodging large rocks and leaping over fallen branches. Tippy wasn't with him. The little traitor had stayed with Vicki because she was making cakes. Danny had left him begging pathetically in the kitchen.

Danny flew over a stump. Twigs, leaves and bark crackled beneath his pounding feet like distant fireworks. 'Sam, waaait! Slow down a bit!' he puffed. 'Wait up!'

Sam kept running. 'No, Danny!' he called back. 'If you can't keep up, go home.'

Danny gritted his teeth. 'I'm not going home!'

'Well, keep up then.'

Danny glanced down into the creek. There were huge trees, dead and grey, lying like the skeletons of dinosaurs. Danny didn't fancy falling on them. He felt dizzy and nearly lost his footing. Stones from under his feet tumbled in a mini avalanche over the edge and bounced down the cliff face. Danny headed away from the edge. 'Don't look down,' he muttered.

Up ahead, Sam stopped at a narrow sheep track that cut down the steep bank. He stood for a moment and looked back through the jigsaw-shadows of the overhanging trees. 'Hurry up!' he called again. Then he looked down to the rocky bed. 'I've found the sheep track. I'm going down.' He squatted and began to slide on his heels.

Danny watched a cloud of red dust rise from his brother's skating feet. Sam's bobbing and shuddering head disappeared into the dust and below the horizon of the creek's bank. Although Danny couldn't see him any more it was obvious from the anguished cry that echoed to the treetops that the momentum of the downhill slide had made Sam go faster than he'd intended.

'Whooooaaa!'

A thicker cloud of powdery red dust rose to the air.

Danny's attention was taken away from his brother when he heard, 'Coooooeeeee!'

Danny lifted his eyes to the call from across the creek. Mark Thompson was on the far side, standing on a high cliff with his arms folded and tapping his right foot impatiently. He lived across the road from Danny and Sam, just down from the Mundowie Hall. This expedition was his idea.

He cupped his hands around his mouth and yelled, 'Get a move on, you guys!' Startled galahs squawked from the trees. Mark was *very* loud.

Danny was puffing hard when he reached the sheep track. He hesitated at the top of the bank. He had a bird's-eye view of Sam running, out of control, arms waving wildly, onto the rocky creek bed. He was screaming and laughing at the same time. 'Aghahahaaaa.'

Amazingly, he didn't fall. Danny smiled thinly and looked down through the veil of his brother's scuffed-up dust. It was a long way down. Rocks jutted from the path and there were tree roots, crooked and claw-like, reaching in from the sides ready to scratch, cut and tear.

Breathing hard, with his toes hanging over the edge of the bank, Danny appraised the sheep track, steeling himself for the descent. He hadn't been this way before. This was Mark's way.

'Come on, Danny!' Mark bellowed impatiently. 'What are you waiting for? The stupid sheep can do it!'

Danny didn't want to be left behind and he didn't want anyone to think he was sillier than the sheep, so he bobbed down, took a deep breath, said, 'Here goes,' and started sliding.

The powdery dust offered no grip. Danny was immediately out of control. He tried to slow himself. He dug his heels in, but the soles of his shoes were well worn. His bum scraped the ground and the sharpest rocks bit into his pudgy flesh. 'Ow! Ow!' He rolled onto his hip. That didn't help. It hurt more. He thought he heard his pants rip. Gritty grains of dirt and muck flew up from his kicking feet and into his gaping mouth. When he closed his mouth he bit down on something soft, round and squashy like a pea. It tasted like sh . . . sheep dung. Yuck! Danny spat furiously.

He reached out desperately and clutched at a tuft of

thick grass, but it was prickly. 'Yeow!' He quickly let it go. Next he snatched at a small bush, but it came right out of the ground – roots and all. Dirt rained down into his hair and eyes. On he skidded with no way to stop, faster and faster, scraping knees and elbows, chewing on dirt and . . . all sorts of things.

Nearing the bottom Danny suddenly thought about the boulders in the creek bed. They made boulder-sized lumps if you headbutted them. The creek bed was looming, but he had a plan. Danny *always* had a plan and this one was simple, well it sounded simple – stand up and run *very* fast. Danny's face was stretched with horrid anticipation. His eyebrows were so high they'd disappeared under his flapping fringe. He prepared himself. Wait for it . . . ready . . . set . . . now!

With only a metre to go to the base of the bank Danny rose quickly to his feet. As if pinged from a slingshot, he flew out onto the creek bed. His stamping feet made the bed of smooth stones snap like clicking fingers. His legs were going far too fast, but there was nothing he could do about it. He waved his arms wildly, desperate not to be overtaken by his own momentum.

Without any real understanding of how it happened, Danny managed to avoid falling flat on his face. He stopped and tried to catch his breath. His legs were like jelly. Stunned, he looked across the creek-bed landscape, past islands of fine creek sand, veins of smooth stones and the grey skeletons of fallen trees. Sam was already scrambling up a dusty slope not as steep as the last toward Mark Thompson.

The far bank was one of Danny's favourite parts of the creek. When the rains came the bank was muddy and slippery, perfect for jumping on an inflated tractor tube and sliding, sometimes flying, down the bank. If there was water in the creek then they would skim across the surface. *Tsh, tsh, tsh*. And then fall in. *Splash!* Danny was convinced that the muddy tube ride was better than any amusement park – although he'd only ever seen the parks on television.

Keen to keep up, Danny ignored any stinging grazes and raced off across the uneven creek bed. His ankles twisted, his cheeks wobbled and the world was shuddering. He reached the other side and looked up to see Sam clamber over the top of the bank and disappear.

Danny started climbing like an ant up a tree trunk. He was out of breath by the time he crawled, grunting and puffing, over the top of the bank and caterpillared into a small forest of tall yellow grasses.

He stood and brushed himself down. A prickle of pain caught his attention. His left knee was stinging.

It was an old injury. He had hurt it riding his bike down the slide in the playground a few days before.

There was a large scab from which a fine thread of blood was trickling. Danny spat on his hand and smeared the dirt, then the blood. He wanted to pull the scab off, but knew it would hurt.

A shadow suddenly loomed over Danny. 'I knew I shouldn't have brought you two. You're slowing me down.'

Danny looked up. Mark Thompson was standing over him.

Mark was a few months older than Sam. He was taller and much bigger. His hair was the colour of the red dust in the creek. Freckles the same colour as his hair were sprinkled across his nose like the rust speckles spattered across the roof of Danny's house. Mark always impressed Danny because he seemed to know everything about everything. *And* he said he could kick a footy right over the Mundowie Hall. Amazing!

Mark looked down at Danny's scab. 'Just pull it off,' he said gruffly. 'If you do it quickly it doesn't hurt.' He looked Danny in the eye. He shaped his fingers into a claw and crinkled his nose. Some of his freckles disappeared into creases. 'Just get your fingernail under the crusty edge and pull.' He looked away quickly. 'I've done it heaps of times.'

That's just what Mark had said when he told Danny to ride his bike down the slide in the playground. *I've done it heaps of times. You can't hurt yourself.* Danny had known it was a stupid thing to do, but he felt as though he had no choice. So he did it. He flew off the end of the slide and went for a spectacular head-over-handlebars tumble. Afterwards, when Mark was laughing at him, he had felt as silly as a sheep. Incredibly, he had only hurt his knee.

Mark leant over and reached for the scab. 'I'll do it for you if you like.'

Danny glanced down at Mark's hands. He shook his head and pulled his knee away. 'No, thanks, I'll leave it for now.'

Mark had big hands, chubby fingers and no fingernails because he chewed them. Grease and grime filled the skin creases in his knuckles. Mark's dad had the same hands. He'd been a farmer like Danny's dad, but not any more. He drove an old truck now and called his business Thompson Transport. He was a big man who loved cowboy hats and country music. He always had black oil or grease stains on his hands. He worked on his truck all the time.

On warm nights Danny and Tippy often sat on the front fence. And when they weren't looking at the stars or the moon or trying to spot frogmouth owls they would look across to Mark's place. The shed doors were often wide open. The radio would be crackling and the interesting percussion of chinking tools drifted out into the night. Mark and his dad would be in there working away on the truck. The soft light, crowded with moths on frenzied flight paths, would reach out across the gravel road. For Danny, looking through the velvet darkness of night to the well-lit shed was like watching a 3-D television set.

'Come on,' Mark whined. 'Let's go. We'll never get to the old Miller place at this rate.'

Mark led the expedition away from the creek. 'You've got to keep up now,' he grumbled. 'I'm not waiting for you again. I'm not your *mother*.'

From the shade of the trees by the creek the path went across an open field and up a hill to where a few sheep were gathering. They all stopped eating grass, lifted their heads and stared at their visitors.

At the top of the hill the boys stood and looked back toward the creek and Mundowie nestled in a gentle hollow in the distance. So did the sheep.

Mark leant on Danny and frowned curiously. 'So why isn't Tippy with you?' he asked.

Danny squinted up at him. 'He's at the funeral with Vicki.'

'Funeral!' gasped Mark. 'Who died?'

'Snot.'

'Snot! Who's Snot?'

'You know, her frog. He's called Snot because he's all blotchy and slimy. She's had him since we caught him as a tadpole in the creek. She caught tadpoles for Sam and me as well, but ours didn't last long enough to become frogs. She was looking after Snot pretty well, but then she forgot about him for a couple of days and didn't put water in his drum, so he got fried. Mum made cakes with her and they're going to bury him near the tractor shed. Tippy stayed, not because he loves Snot but because he loves cakes and knew he'd get some.'

Mark paused thoughtfully then nodded and said, 'Yeah, he's a wise little dog. I know where he's coming from. Your mum's cakes are almost as good as old Mrs Wallace's Anzac biscuits.'

Danny nodded and cast a glance toward the Wallace house. Old Mrs Wallace *did* make pretty good Anzac biscuits. 'We won't miss out on the cakes. Mum will save us some.'

Mark hit Danny on the arm. 'If not we'll go see Mrs Wallace,' he said. 'She's always got a tin full of those biscuits.'

Danny smiled. 'Good idea.'

The roar of a car on the gravel road caught everyone's attention. They saw a familiar white station wagon rumble out of Mundowie. There was a lot of rattling and squeaking. Dust billowed from behind it like smoke from the nostrils of a brooding dragon.

The car roared into the shadows as the road cut

down into the creek. The horn sounded a musical signal. *Bah, dah, dah, dah.*

A hand lifted from the window and waved. Danny waved back. So did Sam.

Mark nudged Sam. 'Where's your dad going?'

'To see the guy at the bank.'

Mark shook his head. The spike of hair that always stuck up between his eyes quivered.

'Huh, my dad hates the bank.'

'Yeah,' said Sam. 'So does ours.'

Danny frowned thoughtfully. He didn't know why his dad hated the bank because the bank gave them money.

'He's just going to get some money,' said Danny. 'The bank guy came to visit him the other day about it.'

Mark leant forward. 'A guy from the bank came to your house?' he asked eagerly.

Danny nodded. 'Yeah, he was a nice guy.'

Mark rolled his eyes. 'Yeah right!' he sneered sarcastically. He turned his back, mumbled something and walked away.

Danny scooted to catch up. Sam and Mark started talking about the old Miller place. It was a tumble-down homestead a couple of kilometres outside of Mundowie. Every kid for miles around said it was haunted. There were stories of two little toddler ghosts wandering around in old-fashioned clothes calling for their mother.

The story was that she had disappeared one day to go walking in the bush and had never come back. Her body was never found. The father was away on farm business. And the kids, home alone, had both been bitten by snakes and died.

Mark Thompson seemed to know more about it than most.

'I've slept out here a couple of times,' he said.

Danny was impressed. 'What, by yourself?'

'Yeah,' Mark shrugged, 'why not?'

'Weren't you scared?'

'No.'

'Did you see anything?'

'Yeah, I saw the kids *and* the mum.'

Danny screwed up his face. 'Jeez, what did they look like?'

Mark stopped and turned. He had a very round face and could make his eyes pop like ping-pong balls. He leant over Danny.

Danny wished he hadn't asked. He hated stories about ghosts and snakes.

Mark made his voice soft and throaty when he said, 'I wasn't scared until I heard . . . the clunk.'

Danny was mesmerised. 'What clunk?'

Mark leant closer, his nose almost touching Danny's.

His glaring right eye was twitching. 'The falling head!' he shouted, as he grabbed Danny by the shoulders suddenly.

Danny jumped back. 'Agggh!' His face was twisted with fear when he asked, 'W . . . w . . . what falling head?'

Mark rolled his eyes. His voice softened again. His right eyebrow arched. 'The mum's head just fell right off when she walked toward me.' Mark clutched at his own neck. 'Aw, it was awful!' He jerked as if pulling his head from his shoulders. 'Then the head was on the floor talking to me asking me if I'd seen her kids. There was blood and bits of skin and veins hanging down from the neck.'

Danny wished Tippy were with him. He looked to Sam. 'We'll be home before dark, won't we?'

Mark chortled. 'You're not scared are you, Danny?'

Danny shook his head hard and straightened himself stiffly. 'No, no I'm not scared. I didn't say I was scared.'

He marched off, leading the way just to prove it. All the while he was wishing he would grow and become brave like Mark Thompson.

There were huge moss rocks on the hill overlooking the Miller homestead. Danny was the first to climb onto them.

A breeze brushed his cheeks. When he dabbed more spit on his scabby knee the coolness made it stop stinging.

To Danny the old homestead was like a castle ruin.

Half the roof was missing. Most of the walls were crumbling; there was no glass in the windows. The rainwater tank was seeping water through rusty veins. There was a windmill that creaked when it turned.

Danny jumped from the rocks. He spied something. He froze and stared hard at a crevice at the base of the boulders. Yes! It was just as he'd thought. There was a freshly shed snakeskin lying there just waiting for him.

Danny loved to hold snakeskins up to his eyes. It was like looking through the cellophane that Vicki used in the eyes of her cardboard glasses. The world looked all soft and dreamy. His dad had shown him one day under the pepper trees down by the tractor shed. Standing at the back fence they had looked across the fields to where the lumpy hills rose to the sky.

Danny dropped to his knees and pushed his arm into the darkness. Mark was curious, so he peered in and saw the skin. He nudged Danny with his knee, unbalancing him.

'He's probably watching you, Danny Allen,' he said.

Danny looked up at Mark's round face, red with the exertion of walking.

'Who?'

'The snake.'

Danny's eyes rolled to the darkness where his hand was fingering the dried skin.

Mark suddenly lunged at him. 'SSStttt!' he hissed, digging three fingers into Danny's shoulder.

Danny flew backwards.

Mark and Sam laughed and ran off toward the homestead.

Danny grabbed the snakeskin and ran to catch up without looking back.

At the old house the stone walls were crumbling.

There were rooms with huge holes in the walls, no doorways and no ceiling. The floorboards were gone and prickly bushes grew in their place.

The boys wandered through, kicking at piles of stones and looking at the carvings on the walls. Danny found one he'd done the last time they'd visited.

Danny Allen was here.

At the back of the house there was only one sheet of rusty iron left on the bull-nose verandah. When a breath of wind came, it would flap.

The backyard was crowded with round prickle bushes. There was one gum tree and two almond trees. The cockatoos loved the almonds. Beyond that there were three huge red sand dunes. An old car wreck and a collection of boulders tangled in large prickle bushes sat in a small valley at the foot of the dunes.

Of the three windswept dunes the middle one was the biggest. The boys called it the Everest Dune. It was much higher than the creek banks. The red sand of the Everest Dune was smooth except for the crinkle of waves made by the wind that brushed its back. Most times, when the boys came to the homestead, they rolled down the steep dunes like tumbleweeds.

But this time, Mark had another idea. He lifted, from beneath some stones, a sheet of iron that had fallen from the verandah. He liked the way it curved at one end. He ignored the cancer of rusty holes.

'Look!' he said, standing the sheet up next to him. 'This is just like a big tin toboggan.'

He lifted his eyes to the top of the Everest Dune. 'I think we should take it and go to the top of the Everest Dune.'

Dropping the sheet of iron to the ground with a clang, he knelt upon it and grasped the upturned end. 'See,' he said, 'we can kneel on this, push each other off and fly down like it was snow. It will be incredible! What do you think?'

Sam looked to the top of the dune then his eyes drifted down to the boulders, the prickle bushes and the old car wreck at the base. He considered the landing. Mark obviously hadn't.

Sam nodded. 'Yeah, all right,' he said wryly. 'That's a good idea, Mark. You go first.'

They trudged up the dune. Mark was excited. 'This thing will fly, I reckon.'

Sam nodded. 'Yeah, I reckon it will.'

'Both of you push me as hard as you can to start me off,' added Mark.

Sam nodded again. 'Yeah, we'll push you hard.'

Danny kept glancing at the rocks. They were huge and very jagged in places. He had to say something; he couldn't keep quiet any longer.

'What about the rocks and that old car at the bottom? How are you going to stop?'

Mark chuckled confidently. 'Oh, I've been on toboggans heaps of times. I know how to stop.'

At the top of the dune there was a breeze. The slope was steeper than it looked from the bottom. Danny stood with Sam as Mark dropped his sheet of iron to the sand. He knelt and took hold of the upturned front. It was rusty and part of it broke off in his hands. He threw it away and grabbed at another spot. The iron was sharp.

'Okay,' he said, shuffling into position. 'When I say go, push as hard as you can and keep pushing until I get up some speed.'

Danny looked down. There was a small mound about a third of the way down. He guessed that if Mark hit that, he was going to get some air. He smiled wickedly at the thought.

Sam tapped Mark on the shoulder. 'If you can't stop, just roll off.'

'Huh! Roll off? No way! *You* can roll off, but I'm not. I know what I'm doing.'

'I hope so.'

'Just shut up and get ready to push.'

'Whatever you say.'

Danny bent over and wrapped his fingers around the end of the iron. The first thing he felt was the softness of the sand. Then, when he closed his grip, he felt the sharpness of the wavy metal digging into his soft palms.

Mark was still shuffling into position. He looked back at Sam. 'This is how you do it, see, you've got to get yourself balanced. You're hopeless; you always lose your balance.'

Sam was getting annoyed, Danny could tell.

Mark continued, 'And you as well, Danny. You only

fell off the slide on your bike because you can't balance. Must run in your family.'

Now Danny was annoyed.

Mark was rocking back and forth on his knees when he said, 'Don't push me until I'm ready.'

Sam looked at Danny and smiled deviously. The smile Danny returned was just as wicked. It was as if they had read each other's mind.

Sam winked at Danny. Danny nodded in recognition of the signal. Mark was still positioning himself when the brothers cried, '*Now!*'

They both ran, pushing hard on the iron. Mark swayed backward and cried out in panic. 'Heeey! No! Not yeeeeeet!'

Too late, he was off. Mark was bouncing and rocking; he hung on desperately. His hair was pushed from his forehead as he gathered speed.

Danny and Sam laughed as they pushed. It was hard work and their feet sank in the soft sand.

Then, as the sheet of iron suddenly dipped forward and headed down the steepest part of the slope, it left their grasp. Away it sped, faster and faster.

Shoooooossshhhhh.

The speed was incredible.

Danny and Sam laughed and stumbled into the softness of the fine red sand, enjoying its warmth.

Danny was astounded at how quickly Mark was

flying down the hill. The sound of the sand shushing beneath the iron was one he would never forget.

Shooo shuuurrrrrooooh.

Danny cringed as Mark's tin toboggan bounced and he saw fine sand spitting into Mark's cheeks. Some must've gone into his mouth because he suddenly began spitting, just as Danny had done himself when skidding down the sheep track.

When Mark repositioned himself so that he was leaning forward and grasping hard, Danny found himself copying the actions.

Danny grabbed Sam by the arm. 'Look at him go!'

Sam laughed as he focused on the flapping of Mark's hair, the bounce of his body and the imagined look of horror on his face.

Mark teetered a little, making the tail of his sheet of iron snake slightly.

'Watch this, watch this,' said Danny, pointing to the small mound that Mark had no hope of avoiding. 'He's going to take off!'

'Whoa, ho, ho, he will too,' chuckled Sam, slapping his knees. 'He'll get some air, all right.'

The brothers laughed hard together as Mark hit the crest of the mound and became airborne. The nose of the iron tipped skyward and Mark leant backward. The tail looked as if it was going to hit the ground and send Mark into a sickening spin.

'He won't land that,' said Sam. 'He's going over.'

Danny held his breath and found himself gritting his teeth waiting for the high-speed tumble.

Incredibly, Mark kept this head and trusted his instinct. Leaning forward, he made the nose dip just enough to level himself.

Thoop!

He made a landing!

It was an awkward landing with a few uncomfortable bounces, but he made it and he continued his ride with the tail of his sheet still snaking.

'Waahhoooo!' he shrieked.

Sam and Danny couldn't help but cheer. 'Yayheeeeeyyyy! Wahooooo!'

Sam looked ahead to the boulders. He wondered if Mark realised how close he was getting. Sam ran from the crest of the dune.

'Look out!' he yelled, his hands cupped around his mouth. 'Look out for the rocks! Get off! Dive!'

Mark didn't respond. He was enjoying the ride.

Danny joined Sam and they shouted together. '*Get oooooff!*'

Mark then quickly started to make sharp body movements. It was obvious that he'd had a sudden realisation of what was coming . . . blood and guts. He rolled frantically onto his side and began jerking hard.

'What's he doing?' Danny cried.

'I think he's trying to turn,' said Sam. 'He's never going to do it. If he hits those boulders or that old car at the bottom, we'll be picking up arms and legs in a minute. His head will be dropping off just like the Miller woman's.'

The image of Mark Thompson's head sitting in the sand with stringy bits of bloodied skin and veins hanging from the neck was burnt immediately into Danny's mind. He strode from the crest of the dune. 'Get off, Thommo!' he bellowed.

Sam started moving quickly down the dune. The sand was soft and his feet sunk to his ankles. He was walking like an emu might walk through sticky mud.

Danny followed. He didn't want Mark to get splattered. The thought of a body standing with bits of skin hanging from a headless neck made him feel worse. Especially if it was someone he knew.

Before Danny could take too many steps he stopped. He stared at Mark, who was now lying on his hip. His hands were pulling at the front of his sheet of iron. With his legs pushing hard and kicking at the tail of his toboggan, Mark tilted hard to one side. He jerked sideways and leant over with all his might and body weight to make his sheet of iron take a wide sweeping turn. It was amazing!

Danny stood and stared as a fine veil of red sand

flew beneath Mark and was pushed skyward. It rose in a long arc; just like a snow skier pushes snow into the air when coming to a stop at the base of a run.

Danny's mouth dropped open as he stood and saw the sun strike the veil, making it glow brilliant orange.

'Wow!' he gasped.

Mark rolled into the sand and sprung to his knees as soon as he stopped. 'Did you see that?' he called, lifting his hands above his head. 'Did you see it?' He was only a couple of metres from the boulders, but he didn't seem to notice. He stood up and began jumping about triumphantly.

'Yeah we saw it,' Sam answered.

Mark pointed to Sam and bellowed. 'Now it's your turn!'

Danny was excited. He jumped through the sand to be by his brother's side. 'This is going to be the best thing ever.'

Sam shrugged his shoulders. He didn't seem excited at all. 'Hmm, maybe.'

Danny was puzzled.

'What do you mean?'

'Well, if we don't do it as well as him we'll never hear the end of it.' Sam motioned toward Mark. 'Just listen to him. If I stuff up, he'll tell everyone how good he was and how useless I am.'

Danny wasn't excited any more. He stood silently next to Sam, rubbing his eyes free of sand.

Sam was right.

Danny didn't know why, but his stomach suddenly fluttered with butterflies. The only time he felt them was when he was nervous, like when Dr Kelly came at him with a needle or the dentist said, 'I just have to drill a little.'

Danny stared at Sam for at least a second and somehow knew that he had butterflies as well. Mark was good at everything and Sam *still* couldn't kick the footy over Mundowie Hall.

Mark was on his way. He was grinning broadly as he trudged up the side of the dune dragging his sheet of iron behind him.

He puffed hard in between short phrases. 'The speed . . . was wicked! Some of the sand . . . spits up and stings you . . . in the face and when I hit that mound, I just . . . went flying. You saw it, didn't you? I thought . . . I was finished, but I wasn't.'

When Mark finally made it to the top he put his hands on Sam's shoulders. 'You *have* to get balanced,' he huffed. 'Or you'll go over before the mound.' He took a few more short sharp breaths. 'Make sure you use your body to do the turn . . . It's easy really. I reckon it is anyway . . . I don't know how you two will go though.'

'We'll be good,' chirped Danny pluckily. 'We know what to do.'

Mark raised his eyebrows and muffled a chuckle. 'Yeah, ha, ha. Well, we'll see.'

He elbowed Sam. 'Are you going first?'

'Yep.'

Mark rolled his eyes. 'This'll be good.'

Sam readied himself for the ride.

Danny found himself giving instructions.

'Be ready for the mound and really lean over hard when you want to do the turn, like Mark.'

'Shut up!' Sam snapped. 'I know what I'm doing. Just you push when I tell you.'

Mark grabbed the back of the iron. The look on his face was fierce. He was going to push with all his might.

Sam shuffled a little. He took a deep breath. 'Okay . . . Push!' he cried.

Danny bowed his head and heaved. Mark grunted. The iron skated across the sand.

Shoowooo, shuuuuuush.

The wind came. Mark was pushing hard, running fast. Danny couldn't stay with him. He was losing his footing. He fell to his knees and felt the iron slip from his grasp.

Mark pushed until Sam went over the edge and down the steepest part of the dune. Mark stood tall, puffing hard. He was smiling when Sam hit the mound.

Sam took off. 'Yaaaghhh!'

He was out of control but ... *thwoop* ... he somehow made a landing.

Danny cheered and clapped. 'Wahhoooo! Go! Go!'

Sam heard him above the whistle and soft howl of the wind around his ears.

Danny bounded down the dune and stood as tall as he could next to Mark. 'He got over the mound pretty well,' he said.

Mark nodded. 'Yeah, but he still has to make the turn.'

Danny stood listening to the sound of his own heart. Sam could do it; he knew he could. He was writhing and twisting now, leaning and rolling. The sheet of iron was lifting at one side. Sam was pulling and jerking. Danny could see how hard he was trying. He could also see how fast he was nearing the boulders.

Danny was about to cry out when Sam gave up and rolled from the iron onto the sand. His arms and legs kicked up a spray of fine sand. Disappointed, he thumped the sand with a fist. The sheet of iron continued the journey and flew over a ridge and onto the tops of the boulders before cannoning into the old car.

Clang!

It twisted sickeningly as it bounced into the air before spinning down again.

Clang! Bang!

'Hey!' Mark yelled. 'There had better not be any dents in that.'

Sam tried to ignore him. He wandered down to collect the sheet of iron, kicking the sand despondently all the way.

The rest of the afternoon they spent taking turns. Danny's first ride was taken with Sam waiting at the bottom in case he couldn't get off near the boulders. Danny was a bit annoyed. He didn't want to be treated like a baby. What would Mark Thompson tell everyone?

But Sam told him he was doing it no matter what. And it was just as well. Sam had to dive at him on one ride and grab Danny's shirt, or he would have been splattered!

Apart from flying down a muddy bank on a tractor tube when the creek was full, the dune ride was the best thing Danny had ever done. The sound of the sand beneath him, the wind making his eyes water, the stinging of the fine grains of sand spitting up and bombing his cheeks. The speed, the way the world shook and shuddered and sped past in a blur. *This*, he thought, *would be like sitting in the space shuttle and being launched*.

Mark Thompson was the best rider. On some of the runs he pushed up a veil of sand as high as the roof on the Miller homestead. No matter how many times Sam tried he couldn't make the turn at the bottom. Mark made it every time with each one being more spectacular than the last. He continued to give Sam tips, of course. 'You just don't know how to bend the knees or use your arms. There's a lot of skill involved.'

Time passed quickly. Shadows grew longer, the sand dune valleys grew darker and the air cooler. The sun took its last peek over the hills and dipped, as if winking, out of sight. The light of the day faded without them noticing. The sand was losing its rich colour to shadow.

Sam was due to have the last ride when Mark Thompson suddenly said, 'Hey, wait up, wait, I've got another idea.'

Danny and Sam exchanged wary glances.

'What now?'

'No listen,' said Mark, grabbing them both. 'I reckon kneeling down is a bit weak.' He parted his legs suddenly and spread his arms. He bobbed on bending knees and said, 'I reckon we should stand on this thing and surf down.' He nodded excitedly. His eyes widened. 'Yeah? What do you think? Come on.'

Sam held the iron and was next to go. He was hesitant. 'Hmm, I don't know . . .'

Mark went to take the iron from him. 'If you're scared, I'll do it.'

Sam tightened his grip on the iron. 'No, it's my go, I'll do it.'

Danny swallowed nervously.

Sam readied himself at the top of the Everest Dune. The horizon was a pastel blend of orange, pink and blue. The air was cool and still. Noise carried easily in echoes. They could hear sheep, magpies, crows and galahs. Sam stood on the iron and took deep breaths. He practised some stances before he put it near the edge. He looked uneasy.

Strangely, so did Mark. He had suddenly started looking at the sky. 'Come on! Get a move on. It'll be dark soon. Look,' he pointed to the sky. 'The first star is out and you still haven't gone.'

Sam looked up and spied Mark's star near the silver-lace moon. 'That's not a star, Thompson, that's Venus.'

Danny was impressed. 'Is it really?'

'Yeah. Lots of people think it's a star, but . . .'

Mark frowned. 'Yeah, that's right, it is. I knew that . . . I remember now. Just get on with it.'

Sam was standing with his arms spread and legs bent. 'Okay, when I say go, push me.' He shuffled his feet. There was a second or two of concentrated silence. Then Sam quietly said, 'Hold it . . .wait . . . hold it . . .'

Mark couldn't stand waiting so he pushed Sam over the edge. 'We can't wait here all night, Allen!'

Sam rocked sharply backward, regained his balance

and slid away. His hips were swaying, his feet shuffling back and forth and his arms flying around his head. He bent his quivering knees. Surprisingly he was still standing when he hit the mound.

The sheet of iron flew through the air. Sam crouched like a real surfer. Danny watched and held his breath as he saw Sam's feet drift from the iron into midair.

Sam crouched low, reached down, grabbed the iron and pulled it back onto his feet like a skateboarder. He landed with a bounce and a snaking twist. He stood again, shuffling his feet and spreading his arms like the wings of a gliding bird.

Danny jumped about and clapped. 'Whaaahhoooo!' he cried, turning to Mark. 'Did you see that? That was brilliant!'

Mark said nothing.

Beyond the mound Sam's hips were still gyrating and his arms weren't waving as wildly as before. Sam was really surfing the dune!

Danny stared, watching every movement. He wished he could see Sam's face. He wished he were on the iron with him.

Danny marvelled at his brother's skill. He had no idea how he was still standing, but as the wind flicked hair across his brow he looked ahead of Sam. Through the blur of watery eyes he saw the boulders.

Sam had to get off . . . or maybe he should try a surfing turn? Mark would find that hard to beat.

The rocks were getting closer . . . closer . . . closer. Danny clenched his fists at his sides as he watched Sam frantically trying to push the tail of the iron into a turn. Sam twisted and jumped, leant and swayed. He was now surfing dangerously close to disaster.

Danny felt his brother's fear.

He ran from the top of the dune. 'Get off, Sam! Juuuump!'

Danny had a vision of threads of blood and skin hanging from Sam's head. Maybe the Miller woman had been surfing the sand dunes when she lost her head.

Danny stood breathless as Sam hit a ridge at the edge of the valley of boulders.

Mark put his hands to his head and gritted his teeth. 'Oh jeez no!'

Danny caught a split-second glimpse of Sam's terrified face as his brother's body spun into the air. Danny had seen highlights on sports shows of surfers being tossed from waves in Hawaii with their bodies twisting and spinning just like Sam's.

Sam flew across the front of the iron. It bounced up before landing beneath him. Sam fell, head first, arms outstretched to break his fall. He fell toward the sharp edge of the iron.

The jagged edges of rusty iron ripped into the softness of Sam's right arm and tore into the flesh of his bicep like angry teeth. 'Aggghhhhh!'

Sam rolled and tumbled. He disappeared over a ridge in a storm of kicked-up sand.

Stunned, Danny and Mark stood as statues. They hoped to see Sam's head, still attached to his body of course, bob up.

A second passed . . . two seconds . . . three seconds . . . nothing. Silence – but for the echo of cockatoos, sheep, crows and magpies.

Mark was the first to speak. 'Jeez. That was some fall. He should be a stunt man.' He turned to Danny. 'I hope he's not dead.'

Danny raced down. His feet stuck in the cool sand, slowing him.

Mark followed.

'He might be knocked out,' said Danny.

'If he's knocked out we have to carry him home,' said Mark. 'We can't stay here in the dark.'

Danny looked back at him. 'But you can stay. You've done it before. You can wait here and I'll go home and get Mum or Dad.'

Mark's face suddenly twisted and crumpled. 'I'm not staying here!'

'You might have to.'

Mark looked across the sand dunes to the darkening corners of the homestead. 'No way! This place is haunted!'

Danny glanced back at Mark again, whose face was buckling – his eyebrows twitching nervously. The fear behind his eyes was obvious. They were darting and blinking wildly.

Danny kept running. 'But you slept here! You're not scared; you said you weren't!'

'No but . . . but . . . I . . . I mean I've done it once and that's enough.'

'But if you *have* to stay, you will, won't you?'

Mark shook his head violently. 'No, I won't! I think we should get out of here as fast as we can. I mean, you see, I don't think *you* should see the headless mum. And if Sam's out to it then we can carry him if we have to.'

Mark was scared and Danny knew it. But it didn't matter.

Danny was puffing hard when he neared the ditch into which Sam had fallen. His heart was pounding as he ran to peer over the edge.

The first thing Danny saw was a patch of redness richer than the sand.

Blood!

Danny's eyes flicked to the glistening flesh of a gaping cut at the top of Sam's right arm. He felt ill looking at it. He thought he was going to cry. The flesh looked just like he imagined the Miller woman's neck might look.

Sam was clutching the gash.

'Help me, Danny, quick.'

Danny jumped to Sam's side. He pushed back big tears. Then came a sound that startled them both. A sad groan followed by . . . *thwump*.

Danny turned sharply, expecting to see a ghost in the half-light of late evening dropping her head at his

feet. But no. He saw Mark Thompson lying flat on his back with his mouth wide open and his arms spread, like a dead person.

'What's wrong with him?' Danny gasped, his eyes darting in all directions. 'It's the ghost, isn't it?'

Sam shook his head. 'No,' he said firmly. 'He's just fainted, that's all. He hates the sight of blood.'

Danny was stunned. 'What? But he said he'd pick my scab and that the woman had blood on her neck and . . . '

'Don't worry about it. You don't believe everything he says.' Sam grimaced. 'Just help me. I need to wrap my arm.' He looked across at Mark. 'Hang on, I know, rip his old T-shirt off and we'll use that. You have to wrap my arm tight, you know, like Mum says if you get snakebite, remember?'

Danny nodded.

He scrambled across the sand to Mark and found a hole in his T-shirt. He stuck his finger in and pulled. As he ripped he glared at Mark. *I bet he's never slept at the homestead*, he thought, *or picked scabs or even ridden down the slide in the playground on his bike.* Danny ripped some more. He didn't understand why Mark told lies. He didn't need to; he could kick a ball over the Mundowie Hall and ride iron down the Everest Dune and make the best turns ever.

Danny ripped long strips of T-shirt off and handed them to Sam. Most of the front of the shirt came away easily.

The sound of the ripping didn't wake Mark. He lay there, his chest and large jelly-like stomach exposed. Gurgling sounds bubbled from his throat occasionally.

Together, Danny and Sam wrapped the wound. Patches of blood stained the cloth like a map.

Sam looked up to the top of the darkening Everest Dune and smiled. 'I can't believe I surfed all the way down.'

Danny grinned. 'Yeah, you looked just like a real surfer, even when you fell.'

Sam nodded. 'Yeah.'

Their next task was to wake Mark.

They looked down at him. His shredded T-shirt hung around his neck. Danny could see the resemblance to Mark's description of the skin hanging from the neck of the headless ghost.

Danny enjoyed slapping Mark's face. He and Sam laughed at how the cheeks wobbled.

Darkness was creeping in fast. The homestead was just a spooky silhouette when they managed to get Mark to his feet.

He didn't mention fainting.

'What happened to my shirt?' he asked drowsily.

'The ghost attacked you,' said Danny.

Mark came quickly to his senses. 'What?'

'Just kidding.'

'We had to use it to wrap this,' said Sam, holding out his arm. 'I might need stitches.'

Mark looked quickly away.

Danny looked at Mark, fascinated by the weird green tinge of his face. 'Ever had stitches, Mark?'

Mark shook his head.

'You know,' Danny continued, pretending to thread a needle, 'they poke a needle into your skin and pull that thread through . . .'

Mark moved away. 'All right! Yep, fine,' he snapped, swallowing uneasily. 'I know! I know!'

They walked quickly over the hills and headed toward the creek. Some of the sheep followed. The sky was the deepest blue that comes just before darkness. The moon was a huge yellow ball sitting above the treetops. Mark kept looking over his shoulder and imagining movement in dark hollows. 'I wish those sheep wouldn't follow us,' he moaned.

Danny had never seen him so twitchy or nervous. Sam wasn't afraid and that made Danny feel brave. He was braver than Mark Thompson and *he* could kick a footy over the Mundowie Hall.

Danny thought about the days ahead and how he could tell the world that his brother had surfed down the Everest Dune and nearly had an arm chopped off. *And* he didn't faint when he saw blood.

Danny smiled to himself. And neither did I, he mused.

He thought that maybe if he and Sam came out and slept at the old Miller homestead one night they wouldn't be scared. Danny wondered if Mark Thompson would come with them.

Danny looked at him waddling a little way ahead. A lone sheep wandered sneakily out of the darkness of a hollow and crept up behind Mark. Mark didn't see it coming.

It bleated loudly. *Baaaaaaaaaaaaaaaaaaahhhhh.*

Mark jumped into the air! 'Eeeeeyaaaaaaggghh!'

Danny didn't know Mark Thompson could jump so high.

Mark ran, kicking angrily at the fleeing sheep. 'You dumb, stupid, idiot animal!'

The sheep was in panic. *Bahhh, bahhh.*

Danny and Sam laughed hard.

At the crest of the hill overlooking the creek the few yellow specks of the lights of Mundowie came into view.

Mark was some way ahead. 'Race you home,' he called. And he was off.

Despite the fact that he had a head start and it wasn't fair, Danny and Sam set off after him. Sam couldn't move as quickly as he'd have liked. His arm hurt. Danny didn't race off. He stayed by his brother's side.

'That's not fair, Thompson!' they called. 'You got a head start!'

They could hear Mark laughing as he raced away. Ghostly white strips of his torn T-shirt fluttered from his round shoulders.

'Losers!' he bellowed.

3
Stanley the Ram

Vicki loved to laugh. 'Ha, ha, ha! Faster, Danny!' she cried. 'Faster. It makes tickly feelings in my stomach. Ha, ha, ha.'

She was perched on the seat of Danny's bike. Danny was standing, pedalling hard. They rode up the driveway and past a crowd of nervous chickens. Tippy was running with the bike. He veered away belligerently and sent the chickens scattering. *Yap, yap, yap.*

Vicki clasped Danny's shoulders like an eagle clasps its prey. Her splayed legs were swaying awkwardly. 'Hit bumps, Dan! Lots of bumps, go on!'

'Don't fall off if I do.'

'I won't.' She gripped harder.

Danny was taking her to the playground to cheer her up. It was his mother's idea. Vicki had been a bit sad for the few days following the death of Snot the frog. But it was over a week since he had died and she was still moping.

Sam told Danny that he thought she was just pretending so that she could get more attention. Early that morning he had been mean. Just after breakfast he told Vicki it was stupid to be so upset over a *frog*. 'That was ages ago; you can't still be upset. He was just a frog, for goodness sake.'

Vicki's retort sounded funny. 'He wasn't just *any* frog,' she said, with hands on hips and neck stretched at Sam like a curious emu. 'He was Snot!'

'Do you mean he was *not*?' Sam chuckled sarcastically. 'Or do you mean he was *Snot*?'

Vicki didn't get it, she was confused. Her lips buckled. 'Don't tease,' she said and ran off.

Danny was happy to cheer her up. Like Vicki, he had felt sad when Snot died and he knew how it felt to be on the receiving end of a cryptic Sam tease.

'Hang on! I'm speeding up,' he called, as he pulled

his bike into the weave of an uneasy zigzag. The wheels rumbled in the gravel.

They went out the driveway and across the road. Vicki swayed and teetered as she laughed. 'Ha, ha, ha. Go, Dan, go.'

Danny was spurred on by the infectious sound of his little sister's laughter. He pumped his legs and hit a pothole on purpose. Vicki bounced into the air. 'Yay! Ha, ha, ha!' She teetered but didn't fall, her grip was so tight.

The bike was old and spattered with dry red mud. The rust spots over the frame were like the freckles on Mark Thompson's nose. Beneath the layers of dust and mud it was metallic blue. It used to be Sam's and before that it had belonged to their older cousin, Matt. Just because it was old it didn't mean it couldn't fly.

The floppy chain rattled and the pedals squeaked in rhythm with Danny's pumping legs. 'Hang on, Vicki,' he called. 'We're going to hit another pothole!' Danny imagined her face and smiled to himself. He lunged forward, gripped the handlebars until his knuckles were white and gave an extra hard push.

Vicki clung on. They hit the hole. Everything rattled and shook. With a little wobble and a lot of laughing, they continued down the gentle slope on the far side of the road. Danny crouched low over his handlebars like the cyclists in the Olympics. He pushed his legs with all his might. Vicki threw her head back and let the wind lift her fine long hair, the same colour as Danny's, from her shoulders.

They rode past the Mundowie Hall. Vicki waved to the soldier statue that stood guard at the front. 'Hellooooo soldier statue man.'

Tippy stopped for a sniff on the steps of the hall.

'Tippy!' Vicki called. 'Keep up, come on!'

He ignored her. The smell, whatever it was, was too disgustingly luscious. He lifted his leg and left a message for any other dog that might pass by – this was his town and they needed to know. Then he took off again. He was so fast, his little muscles were firm and his legs a blur. He caught up in no time. *Yap, yap, yap.*

Danny suddenly turned sharply and changed direction. Vicki nearly slid off the seat. 'Whooooa!'

'We'll go the long way,' Danny called.

'Yeah!'

The route Danny chose took them along the main gravel road . . . past Thommo's house and the church . . . then round a corner and past the cemetery. The Wallaces (old people like Danny's grandparents) lived near the cemetery and right next door to the playground.

Mrs Wallace was a squat little lady with a 'sunshine smile', Danny's mum called it – so big and broad that it lit up her whole face. Her hair was as white as white and she wore it the same way every day – short and curled perfectly at her shoulders. She was famous for her cooking. Her meringues were good, but Danny agreed with Mark Thompson's assessment that she made the best Anzac biscuits in the world.

Danny, Vicki and Sam called her Aunty Jean although she wasn't their aunt at all. She was very friendly and kind, not only to the children but to Danny's mum as well, who was often over visiting Mrs Wallace for a cup of tea and a biscuit.

Mr Wallace was taller and much rounder than Mrs Wallace. Too many Anzac biscuits was Danny's guess . . . but she also made cake with thick, real melted-chocolate icing; maybe that was it.

As Danny sped past the cemetery Tippy ran off in search of rabbits. There were a lot of holes between the headstones. Danny felt sorry for the rabbits having to share a hole with dead people. Their little rabbit lounge room could very well be inside the rib cage of a skeleton. Or inside a coffin with a wormy, decomposed body, like that of old Mr Adams, who had died only two weeks before. Danny didn't like to think about it, but sometimes his imagination, helped by gory TV shows, was just too strong.

Vicki's hand wrapped suddenly around his throat, pulling him backward and taking his mind off revolting rabbit houses in cemeteries.

'You're choking me, Vicki!'

'Ha, ha, ha. Sorry, I nearly fell off.'

When the Wallace house came into view Danny spied Sam and Mark. They were standing at the sheep pen beside the Wallaces' driveway. They were pointing and laughing at something.

Danny pulled up next to them in what he thought was an impressive skid. Dust rose from his wheel. Vicki slid awkwardly from her seat. 'Whoops!'

Sam and Mark took no notice.

Vicki wiped her eyes with a laugh and pulled at her hair. 'Thanks for the ride, Dan.'

She skipped off to the playground, singing. She paused and turned. 'You can take me back later.' Then, without waiting for confirmation of her taxi booking home, she continued happily on her way. *Tra, la, la, la, la.*

Danny dropped his bike and walked up to the boys. 'What are you doing?'

Sam pointed through the tall wire fence. 'Look at that.'

Danny clasped the wire and looked into the paddock. There was a huge ram staring back at the boys. He was massive, with a thick woolly brow and huge horns.

'Wow! He's huge,' said Danny.

'You know who that is, don't you?' asked Sam.

'Who?' asked Danny.

'That's Stanley,' said Sam.

'Stanley?' gasped Danny. 'It is not! It can't be.'

Mark nodded firmly. 'It is!'

'But look at him.'

'Yeah,' said Sam, wrapping his fingers in the wire of the fence and leaning. 'What did you feed him when he was little, Anzac biscuits?'

Mark laughed.

Danny couldn't believe his eyes. He had known Stanley when he was just a lamb. Something terrible had happened to his mum and she had died in a paddock.

Danny didn't like to think of life without a mum. He had felt sorry for Stanley, and Mr Wallace didn't want to lose him. 'I need all the stock I can get,' he had said. So Danny had helped Aunty Jean look after the little lamb. He was fluffy and hilariously clumsy, always tumbling over. Danny carried him a lot.

When it was time for a feed they would sit on the front step of Aunty Jean's verandah. Danny would eat biscuits dunked in cups of farm-fresh milk and feed Stanley with a bottle.

Aunty Jean had put the finger of a rubber glove on the end and pricked the tip with a pin. Danny had to hold it still while little Stanley attacked it. He loved his milk and always gripped the bottle as if he were starving. His tail would spin like a helicopter blade and Danny would laugh at him.

After feeding they would sometimes play roly-poly games in long grass. After a while, for some reason, probably because of school, Danny and Stanley had lost contact.

Standing at the fence gazing in at Stanley, Danny remembered him being a strong little lamb but he had had no idea he would grow to be so big. His horns were massive. His wool curled tightly into a healthy thatch on his head. He looked pretty good for a little ram that had never had a mum.

'He's awesome!' said Danny, sounding like a proud father. 'I'm going in to see him.'

Mark grabbed Danny's arm. 'Don't be stupid! He'll tear you to shreds.'

Danny pulled away from Mark's grasp. 'No he won't, he'll remember me.'

Mark laughed mockingly. 'Don't be an idiot! Sheep can't remember things! He'll tear you apart if you go near him.'

'How come you're so sure he'll attack me?'

'Because he's mad,' said Mark.

Danny tilted his head curiously. 'Mad?'

'Yeah, haven't you heard?' Mark continued. 'The kids on the school bus were telling me how wild he can be.'

'I didn't hear anyone say that.'

'You don't sit up the back.'

'Who told you then?'

'Ernie Critchley. He told me that when Stanley was in the paddock near their farm he hid behind a tree and waited for Ernie's dad to ride past on his motorbike. Then Stanley charged out of nowhere and knocked Ernie's dad right off the bike and sent him flying into the creek. Then he attacked the motorbike, punctured both tyres and walked off with the petrol tank stuck on the end of one of his horns like a trophy.'

Danny pictured Stanley in hiding and then Mr Critchley flying into the creek. That would be some feat. Mr Critchley was a *giant* of a man with hands the size of frisbees.

'Yep,' nodded Mark learnedly. 'Stanley here is a bit of a renegade. He attacks anyone that comes near him. Apparently he butted old Mr Wallace and threw him up into the air with a single flick of his head. The poor bloke flew clean over his tomato patch, spinning and twisting. He landed flat on his back under the apple tree near his rainwater tank. That's why he's got a walking stick now.'

Danny put his fingers through the wire fence and clung on. He peered in at Stanley. He looked strong but he didn't look mean.

Danny didn't take his eyes off the big ram when he said, 'I don't believe you, Mark. He wouldn't hurt anybody. He's as gentle as a . . . lamb. I know because I used to feed him.'

Mark picked up a stick. 'Oh yeah? Watch this.' He moved back a little from the fence and threw it at Stanley.

'Hey!' Danny cried. 'Don't do that!'

The stick hit the ram between the eyes. He snorted and lowered his head before charging clumsily at the fence. The boys all jumped back as Stanley headbutted the fence with a dust-stirring skid.

'See!' said Mark. 'He's mad. He's a menace. If he got out of there, he'd kill someone.'

With his brow deeply furrowed, Danny marched right up to Mark Thompson. 'I bet you'd go mad too if some *idiot* threw a stick at you!'

Mark lifted his shoulders and frowned darkly. 'What did you call me?'

Danny had never stood up to Mark Thompson before. He usually backed down. But not this time.

'You heard me,' said Danny, thrusting his neck forward like a turtle. 'Don't tease him.'

They glared at each other.

Sam broke the tension. 'Look out! Here he comes again!'

Stanley thrust his head at the fence for a second time. The tip of one of his curling horns became caught in the wire. Distressed, Stanley pulled wildly, twisting and shaking his head, trying to break free. The wire was tangled tightly. Mark laughed at Stanley's frantic attempts to pull free. The fence rattled and shook.

Danny lunged forward. He reached out to the wild whipping of the sharp horns.

'Danny!' Sam cried. 'Get back!'

Danny ignored him. He pulled at the fence, grabbed at the sharp horn and unravelled the wire. Stanley was free. Danny pedalled backwards, lost his balance and fell to the ground.

The huge ram snorted and spun himself, kicking and bucking, in a swelling cloud of red dust. Then he was suddenly calm and stared back at the boys.

'Now leave him alone!' Danny bellowed. 'You'd better hope he doesn't have a memory, Mark, because if he gets out of there he'll have you.'

'You're as mad as that stupid ram, Danny Allen,' said Mark, pushing a foot into Danny's leg.

Sam grabbed at Mark's grease-stained shirt. 'Come on, Thommo, let's go kick the footy. Maybe we can kick it over the hall.'

Mark Thompson turned sharply to Sam. 'I don't think so. There's no way you'll get it over the hall!'

'You never know, I might today.'

'Huh, no chance. *No* chance! Let's just kick it between the trees near the statue. My hamstrings are sore anyway and I won't be able to kick too well today.'

Sam and Mark walked away squabbling.

Danny stayed with Stanley. As soon as the boys were out of earshot he talked softly to him. 'Remember me, Stanley? I used to feed you.' The ram seemed to be listening. 'I gave you milk. You've got to remember me.'

Stanley turned away and walked back toward the homestead.

Danny watched him until he heard Vicki call. 'Hurry up, Danny! You've got to push me.'

Vicki was waiting in the playground. She was sitting on a swing that had a bright blue seat. 'Look, Danny!'

she cried. 'A new seat! Dad put a new seat on the swing.'

'No, he didn't,' said Danny. 'He painted it, that's all. He's going to paint the others in the next few days.'

Vicki touched the seat as if it were gold. 'It looks new.'

Danny's dad had been working on the playground. After a long day in the paddocks he had worked in the last light of the evening. He had a welder and had been a carpenter before becoming a farmer. The council had asked him to help fix the old playground. Danny's dad said he could use the extra money so agreed to help out. Danny liked the sound of extra money. He thought he might ask for a new bike. He wanted a silver one that could do jumps. He wanted to ride cross-country down through the creek without having to worry about chains falling off, or pedals breaking.

Vicki was sitting on the swing dangling her legs. 'Push me, Danny! Push me. Come on. I want to fly like you and Sam do on the swings.'

Vicki didn't know how to make a swing fly. She was good at twisting them to make them spin her dizzy though. She told Danny he was the best swing flyer she'd ever seen. He knew she was lying. Sam was the best. He could make a swing fly so high he almost swung in a complete circle. 'Teach me how to fly like you, Danny,' she pleaded.

Danny tried to explain to Vicki how to move her legs back and forth with the movement of the swing. She was hopeless. She either kicked her legs too much or at the wrong time. Danny tried for almost half an hour and she still couldn't do it.

He jumped onto the swing with the splintery seat next to her. 'Look, watch me.' He started swinging. Vicki watched intently.

'All you have to do,' Danny continued, 'is move your legs with the swing. So when you go forward you push your legs out straight . . . see . . . and when you go backwards you tuck them under. See . . . it's easy.'

Vicki nodded enthusiastically. 'Okay, now I get it.'

Danny heard a car and turned to see Mr and Mrs Wallace pull out of their driveway. They stopped at the gate. Aunty Jean rolled her window down. 'Hi kids,' she called. 'How did your dad go with the bank, Danny?'

Danny didn't know, but he gave an answer that made sense to him. 'He got more money like always, Aunty Jean.'

Aunty Jean turned to her husband and said something that Danny couldn't hear. Then she waved. 'See you then.' The car pulled slowly away.

'Watch me, Danny!' Vicki cried. 'You have to watch me.'

Danny turned back to his sister.

Vicki concentrated hard on her swinging, so much so that her tongue stuck out of the side of her mouth. She tried and tried but couldn't get it. Her swing just wobbled from side to side.

Danny sighed. He couldn't be bothered. 'You'll get it, just practise for a while.'

He set his swing in motion, pushed hard and took off. As he gained height he peered across to the Wallaces' to see if he could spy Stanley. The paddock looked empty. Danny thought nothing more of it and turned back to enjoy the feeling of flying. He stuck his arms out like wings and pretended he was gliding.

As soon as he was as high as he could go he closed his eyes. It was a great feeling – it was like a dream.

Danny was enjoying himself until he heard frantic voices calling in the distance. The sounds of obvious panic aroused his curiosity. He opened his eyes. The wind whistling past his ears made the voices seem farther away than they actually were, but he recognised them straightaway.

First he heard Mark Thompson.

'Run! Hurry up! He's gaining on us! Ruuuun!'

Then he heard Sam.

'You shouldn't have teased him!'

'He's mad!'

'He is now, thanks to you!'

Danny slowed his swing and tracked the voices. They were coming from the other side of the cemetery.

By the time Danny had stopped his swing Vicki was at the playground fence peering up the street to see what all the fuss was about. Danny ran to join her. That's when everything became clear.

Sam was the first to appear, sprinting around the corner. His arms and legs were pumping furiously. Hot on his heels was Mark Thompson. He might be able to kick a footy over the Mundowie Hall, but he was not a fast runner.

He looked clumsy and as if he were about to take a tumble with every step. His round cheeks were wobbling violently. His face was red and he was huffing and puffing loudly.

The running style he used was funny to watch. He pulled his shoulders back and thrust his barrel chest out. His round knees came up very high. The way he pushed his chin into his chest made it look as if he didn't have a neck. His eyes were bulging to an incredible size. And his whole body quivered with the pounding of his large feet. 'Look out! Look out!' he bellowed.

Mark looked continually over his shoulder. Danny wasn't sure why, until he saw what the boys were escaping. Stanley appeared. Danny would never have believed a ram could have such focus. He wanted those boys.

Vicki smiled when she saw Sam and Mark racing. Her smile broadened when she saw Stanley charging after them. She didn't understand the seriousness of the situation. Having watched her brothers at sports days, she thought that whenever people ran fast the idea was for the crowd watching to jump up and down and cheer. So she did.

'Run, Sam! Go! You can win! You can win!'

When she saw Stanley she pointed, laughed and cried out, bouncing up and down like a ball. 'Ha, ha, a ram race! A ram race! Yay!'

Danny leant over the playground fence. 'In here, Sam!' he cried, waving madly. 'Run in here! Quick! We can hide in the fort.'

The playground had an old wooden cubby house. Everyone called it the fort. It was hardly a fort but *fort* sounded better than *cubby house*. Mark Thompson took the credit for the name. He was never going to be a party to anything called a *cubby house*.

With no other plan in place Sam took Danny's advice. Mark was not far behind, but he was slowing. 'Wait for me! Wait!'

Stanley was tossing his head menacingly.

Danny grabbed Vicki's arm and stopped her from cheering. 'Get into the fort! Quick!'

'Why? I want to watch to see who wins.'

'Sam wins, now run for the fort.'

'How do you know?'

Danny pulled Vicki from the fence. 'I said run to the fort! Do as I say. I don't want another day like the one at the dam.'

Vicki put her hands on her hips and frowned defiantly. 'What do you mean?'

Danny looked her in the eye. 'Well, if Stanley the giant ram spears you with his horns he'll rip your guts out!'

Vicki threw a quick glance at the size of the horns. She put a hand on her stomach. She suddenly realised what was happening. 'I'm scared, Danny,' she cried, tugging at her brother's shirt. 'You come with me!'

'I will! I will! When Sam gets here.'

'Me too,' said Vicki, clutching Danny's hand. 'I'll wait for Sam.'

Sam arrived and ran straight past Danny and Vicki. 'Come on!' he panted. 'Over to the fort! Hurry up!'

Vicki wouldn't let go of Danny's hand. They ran toward the fort and Vicki trailed behind like the tail of a kite in a wild wind.

Behind them they could hear the puffing and blowing of Mark Thompson. 'Wait up!'

Danny, Vicki and Sam were at the fort peering out the little window when they saw Mark stumble at the gateway of the playground. Grabbing hold of the gatepost he tripped and, with a violent twist of his tired body, fell to the ground. If there was a gate to shut, he would've been safe, but there wasn't.

Stanley saw the fall. He eyed the body on the ground and closed in.

Sam stuck his head out of the fort window. 'Thompson! Get up!'

Mark didn't need to be told. He was trying to get to his feet, but his legs were like jelly and he was out of breath. He lifted a hand and reached out desperately for help that wasn't there. 'Come and help me!'

Mark rose to his knees and was on all fours. Stanley was right behind him. Mark's large round bum, wobbling and shuddering, was a perfect target. Stanley dipped his head and ran hard. The contact he made must have given him great satisfaction. *Thoomp!* He butted the huge target with fantastic force.

Mark was thrown sharply forward. 'Agghh!' His head struck a rock. *Crack!* The sound was sickening. Then he lay, flat and still, not moving at all.

The hostages in the fort fell silent. They stared, waiting and hoping for movement. There was none; Mark looked dead.

'What happened back there, Sam?' asked Danny. 'How did Stanley get out?'

'Mr Wallace must have left a gate open,' Sam panted. 'Stanley was near the hall munching grass. He was wandering about quite happily minding his own business until Mark saw him and decided to kick the footy at him. The ball hit the ram in the face and, naturally, Stanley wanted to kill him.'

'Well, he might have,' gasped Danny, motioning toward Mark's body. 'He hasn't moved, so he's either unconscious or dead!' Danny started to stand. 'We have to help him.'

Sam grabbed him. 'We can't go out there! You saw what that mad animal did to Thommo.'

Vicki shook her head worriedly. 'No, Danny, you can't go out there. I don't like guts coming out.'

'Everyone shout,' Sam suggested. 'Someone might hear us.'

'Who?' said Danny. 'Mr and Mrs Wallace aren't home. I saw them go out in the car.' He looked around. 'And I don't think anyone in the cemetery will hear us.'

'Where's Tippy?' asked Sam.

'I don't know. He went off sniffing for something,' said Danny.

'Well call him, he'll help us.'

'No way!' protested Danny. 'He's too little. Stanley would kill him with one blow.'

At that moment Stanley thrust his horns grumpily at Mark again. He lay still and floppy. Stanley butted him again. Mark was pushed onto his back. The gash on his forehead where he had hit the rock became visible. It glistened.

Danny couldn't stand watching any more. 'I'm going to help him.'

Sam pushed a stiff arm across Danny's chest, barring his exit. 'Don't be stupid!'

Danny pushed the arm away. 'Stanley won't hurt me. I used to feed him.'

Sam shook his head. 'Sheep can't remember things!'

Danny put his hands firmly on his hips. 'They know where all the best tracks in the creek are and how to get there. If they can remember that, then Stanley will remember me. It wasn't *that* long ago that I used to nurse and feed him.' Danny pointed in Mark's direction. 'And I have never teased him. I bet he remembered Mark. Stanley's got no reason to be angry with me.'

Before Sam could respond, Danny suddenly darted from the fort. Once out of the reach of his protesting brother he slowed down to a sneaking pace.

'Don't go, Danny!' Vicki cried through the small window. 'Come back in. Come back in!'

'Yeah, don't be an idiot, Danny,' Sam called. 'Get back here.'

'He won't hurt me,' said Danny out of the corner of his mouth. 'I know he won't.'

'You don't know anything, Danny,' said Sam. 'He's not a lamb any more. He's mad!'

Vicki put some hair into her mouth and started chewing nervously. 'Daaannnyyyy,' she whined.

Sam watched silently. In his mind he ran through some strategies of what to do if Danny found himself in trouble. He would have to grab a big stick and charge.

Danny stood in the playground and called gently to Stanley. 'Hey, Stanley boy, hey?'

He scooped up a handful of soft, powdery dust. He threw it into the air to attract Stanley's attention. It drifted in a cloud over the ram's head.

Mark Thompson lay still, as if dead. The gash on his head looked disgusting. For an instant, Danny gained some wicked satisfaction at seeing the gash. Mark would need stitches and he didn't like stitches. He couldn't even look at Sam's arm when he'd had stitches after the dune surfing. He even hated seeing the scar they'd left. Anyway, getting stitches would serve him right!

Stanley looked up to the dust Danny had thrown. The big ram stepped back. He turned to look at Danny. Their eyes met.

'Please come back in, Danny!' Vicki cried.

Danny bent down and pulled up a big tuft of green grass that was growing around the base of the playground tap.

He held it out and offered it to Stanley. The big ram tossed his head once . . . then twice.

Danny's heart thumped hard against his chest. Stanley eyed him. Danny froze. Danny was sure he was going to charge. So was Sam. He moved to stand just outside the fort. Vicki held her breath.

Stanley started to walk toward Danny, who didn't flinch.

'Keep still, Danny,' Sam urged.

Danny waved the grass tentatively. Stanley kept coming: slowly, cautiously, suspiciously.

'Here, boy,' said Danny nervously. 'Have some grass.'

Sam picked up a stick ready to charge at the big ram and beat him away if he took to Danny. Vicki turned away; she couldn't watch. 'I don't like to see guts,' she mumbled forlornly to herself.

Danny offered the grass cautiously to Stanley's nose.

The ram sniffed and took a cautious step forward.

He then began nibbling sedately. Danny knelt and pulled up more grass. A minute later he had a hand on Stanley's back as the big ram munched happily at the small forest of grass around the tap.

Danny looked to Sam. 'The grass should keep him busy. Come on, let's drag Thommo out of the way.'

Sam moved slowly to stand with Danny. 'If Stanley looks like having a go at us,' he said, 'we get back in the fort.'

Danny nodded.

Vicki called to her brothers. 'What about me?' she squealed. 'Don't leave me here, dooooon't.'

'You wait. We'll get you in a minute.'

'But I . . .'

'No buts. Just wait in the fort and *don't* come out. Got it?'

Vicki nodded. 'Well, hurry up then,' she whined.

Sam and Danny stood side by side. Staying close together they crept across the playground. Sam clutched his stick, ready to strike, just in case.

They reached Mark without any problems. Stanley hadn't even noticed them. The grass was good on this side of the fence.

Mark was moaning when the brothers knelt at his side. He stirred as Sam moved to look at the gash.

'What? Who?' Mark mumbled incoherently. He lifted his head. 'Where is the . . .? Oh, my head hurts.'

Danny stuck a hand over Mark's mouth. 'Shhh!'

Sam looked at the gash and screwed up his face. 'That's horrible,' he said.

Mark's head fell to the ground with a thud and he groaned again.

'Come on, hurry up and grab his arms,' said Danny. 'We'll have to drag him.'

Sam grabbed an arm and they began dragging. Mark's head wobbled and his body left a wide trail. He opened his eyes. 'What . . . what are you doing?' he asked dozily. 'Get off me! I can . . .'

'You can't do anything!' hissed Danny. 'Just shut up!'

'Yeah shut up!' Sam agreed.

They dragged Mark into the fort and sat him up. He suddenly remembered what had happened. 'Oh no! Where is that beast? Where is it?'

'He's over there,' said Danny.

Stanley looked so peaceful and harmless. He occasionally lifted his head and gazed around as he munched.

The children took the opportunity to slink out of the playground. Danny and Sam supported Mark all the way. At the Mundowie Hall they stopped to sit at the feet of the soldier statue and rest. Sam looked at Mark's head. It wasn't as bad as it had first seemed. 'We'd better get you home. Your mum will have to take you to the hospital in Port Bilton.'

Danny grinned wryly when he said, 'You might need stitches.'

Sam lifted the arm of his shirt to show the scar from the cut he'd got when surfing the Everest Dune. 'You won't need nine like me though.'

Mark bowed his head and buried his face in his hands. 'No, I won't need any, I won't.' He babbled incoherently. 'If I do, I'll need ten at least. But they're not poking a needle and thread into me.'

'It's okay,' said Danny, keen to make Mark as uncomfortable as he'd made Stanley. 'I watched them do Sam. They push the needle into your skin and when they pull the huge silver needle through,' (Danny pinched his skin on his arm and stretched it) 'your skin stretches up and . . .'

'Shut up!' Mark grumbled. He went suddenly pale and hung his head again. 'And anyway, my mum's not home.'

'Where is she?' asked Vicki, looking up at the soldier and the sky beyond. She hated blood as well.

'She's in the city.'

Vicki scrunched up her face and closed one eye to find out if she could see up the nose of the soldier statue. 'Why?' she asked matter-of-factly.

Mark paused. 'She's looking for somewhere to live.'

Vicki opened both eyes and looked quickly at Mark. 'Are you moving away, Mark Thompson?'

Mark didn't respond immediately. Vicki nudged him. 'Well? Are you?'

Mark shook his head. 'No . . . just my mum,' he answered softly.

There was silence.

Vicki fired another innocent question. 'What about your dad?'

There was another pause. '. . . Nah, he says he hates the city.'

'But that means they'll live in different houses, doesn't it?'

Sam hit Vicki on the arm. 'Stop asking so many questions, Vicki. We have to get home.'

Sam helped Mark to his feet. 'I tell you what, Thommo, if your dad can't take you to Port Bilton then my mum or dad will. You have to be checked for concussion at least.'

Mark didn't say anything except, 'Jeez my head hurts.'

◆

A few days later Danny was at the playground again. Vicki was there as well trying to fly on the swing. Sam had gone with Mark and his mum to get Mark's four stitches out.

It was late in the evening. The sky over Mundowie

was streaked with a wash of wispy orange clouds. Danny was helping his dad. They were sanding down splintery swing seats and painting them blue. Danny suddenly thought it might be a good time to ask about the extra money and the silver bike.

But then his father stopped painting and said, 'With this extra money I can get some work done on the old tractor.' He looked into the paint tin he was holding. 'And I'll tell you what, Danny. We'll spruce up your bike if there's any of this paint left over. We'll make it sparkle, Danny boy, just like new.'

Danny looked up at his dad. He was smiling and he was wearing the hat with the broad brim, the brown leather lining and the grease mark on the top that looked like a map of Africa. He tipped it back off his forehead. He looked to the sky. 'If we can just hang on for another year, things have to come good. The last few years have been tough, so I'd gamble on the next season being a better one. With enough rain and a bumper crop we'll get a new tractor *and* a new bike.' His father ruffled his hair. 'How would that be, Danny boy?' he said brightly.

Danny nodded and smiled. 'Yeah, that'll be good, Dad.'

'Yeah,' said his father distantly, 'if we can just convince them to let us hang on.'

'Who, Dad?'

'Ah, never mind, Danny, let's get this playground sparkling.'

When Danny looked to the sky, he wished for days of thunder and rain just like the day he went on the secret mission of tadpole hunting in the dam. That's what he was thinking about when the sound of a car caught his attention. Mr Wallace was pulling out of his dusty driveway. He was towing a trailer with high wire sides that made it look like a cage. There was a large animal in the trailer. Danny stared as the trailer came clearly into view. The large animal was Stanley. He was riding in the back. Danny and his dad waved. Mr Wallace tooted his horn and pulled away.

Stanley was staring out of the back of the trailer. From where Danny was standing, Stanley seemed to be staring right at him. Danny watched him until he was lost in a cloud of dust and the fading light of the closing of another day.

Danny stopped painting. 'Where are they taking Stanley, Dad?'

'He's been sold to another farm for breeding. He's moving out of Mundowie and on to bigger things.'

Danny couldn't imagine moving out of Mundowie.

'Mr Wallace is pretty chuffed about it all actually,' his dad continued, pushing his hat thoughtfully from his brow again. 'He got a good price for him. He hadn't thought Stanley would ever amount to much, but there you go, you can never tell.'

'So Stanley's done all right for himself, Dad?'

'Yep, he certainly has; and they don't call him Stanley any more. That name just doesn't sound important enough for such a proud and stately animal.'

'What do they call him?'

'Solomon.'

'Solomon?'

'Hmm, that's right, one of the great wise kings of long ago.'

Danny stood and smiled to himself. He felt good

inside. He had helped nurture a great king. A king with the wisdom to attack kids who kicked footballs at him, but not kids who fed him milk when he was little. The more Danny thought about it, the more he became convinced of just how special Stanley really was. Still, deep down inside, where his fondest memories of Stanley the lamb lingered, he had always known it to be true.

The sun had set and the sky was losing its colour and Venus was twinkling when Danny, Vicki and their dad left the playground.

At the gateway to the playground Danny found a thick tuft of Stanley's wool snagged on some wire. Danny pulled it free and tucked it into his pocket. He felt it all the way home. As they walked Danny's dad talked about fixing the tractor, mending the plough and cleaning Danny's bike ready for painting.

When they neared the house Danny looked across the street. The light was on in Mark Thompson's garage. The chink of tools blended with the echo of the radio. Mark's dad was alone. He was under the truck fixing something as usual. Danny could only see his legs. There was no car at the front of the house.

When Danny got inside he followed his dad down the passageway. Tippy was back from his smelling expedition and came running from the kitchen to greet them. He'd rolled in something revolting. He stunk! They walked into the kitchen with Tippy leaping and springing happily. The radio was loud. Danny noticed that it was on a different station to the one in Mark Thompson's shed.

He watched as his dad took his mum and swirled her about. They laughed together.

Smiling to himself, Danny jumped up onto a stool to sit and watch.

The radio played and they danced a silly dance. They laughed loudly. Tippy barked and the kitchen was warm.

4

Running Away

The mouth-watering smells of freshly baked cakes and biscuits drew Danny into the kitchen. His mum was having a cooking day. She had her back to Danny and was at the table kneading dough. The radio was on and her hips were swaying. Danny noted that she was wearing the apron she wore the day Vicki went tadpole hunting in the dam. The thought of that day made the hairs on the back of his neck prickle.

He lifted his nose to the air and took a *big*

breath . . . ahhhh! There was nothing better than the smell of warm cakes, biscuits or freshly baked bread . . . except maybe the smell of rain on a really hot day . . . or the freshly cut wheat when his dad was harvesting.

Danny wandered the kitchen like an archaeologist searching for treasures inside a pharaoh's tomb. There was a tray of biscuits cooling on top of the cupboard near the fridge, well out of reach.

Small cupcakes were rising in the oven and the dough his mum was kneading was for bread. She always made the tall loaves with round, light brown crusty tops. Everywhere Danny looked, he saw dirty dishes and mixing bowls stacked in leaning towers. They reminded him of the ruins of an ancient city.

He wandered past the ancient city of bowls and plates, peeping between the towers into small alleyways. Large spoons dripped with stalactites of cake mix. Eyeing his mother shiftily, Danny scraped some mixture off a spoon with his finger and popped it in his mouth.

'Grubby fingers out, Danny Allen!' his mother scolded.

Danny jumped. Astonished, he looked at her. She still had her back turned. How did she see him do that? Danny should've known better, that's what his mum always said when he did something stupid, like riding a bike down the slide in the playground. It seemed no matter what he did and no matter how good a secret he thought he had, she found out, somehow.

'Tastes good, Mum,' he said, walking over to the table.

Danny's mum was singing the Beatles' song *Love Me Do* quietly as she kneaded and swayed in time with the music.

She looked up, stopped singing and smiled. She widened her eyes. 'We'll have a feast of warm bread, butter, honey and jam later.'

She was good at making the simplest things sound exciting. Danny couldn't wait.

He leant his elbows on the table and with his face cupped in his hands he gazed up at her. She had flour in her hair around her temples. Like grey hair – it made her look old. Danny didn't mention it.

Danny found himself mesmerised by the nimble movement of his mum's thin fingers writhing through the dough. She tugged at it and it stretched like elastic. Danny thought of Mark Thompson's skin when he had to go to the hospital in Port Bilton to get stitches in his head.

He smiled reflectively at the thought. He wished he'd been there. Sam said it was brilliant. One of the most spectacular things he'd ever seen. Amazingly, Mark didn't faint. But he *did* throw up all over the doctor, on his white coat and his suede shoes, everywhere –

carrots, peas and chunks of mince, everything. Sam's description of the contents was very graphic. Danny blocked the thought for fear of it putting him off the feast he had been promised.

Danny's mum suddenly pulled a small piece of dough into her hands and began rolling it in her palms. She shaped it to the size of a tennis ball and bowled it slowly across the table to Danny, who stopped it with a flat hand.

'What's this for, Mum?'

'Why don't you make something?' she suggested, pushing hair from her forehead with the back of her hand. 'I'll bake it for you.'

Danny took the dough in his hands and frowned curiously. 'What should I make?' he asked.

'If you make a head with a face and hair it will look funny when it's baked.' She made a weird face by puffing up her cheeks and making her sparkling eyes bulge. 'Everything will puff up,' she said, pushing her funny face close to Danny's.

Danny chuckled. 'Okay then,' he said. 'I *will* make a head.'

Danny set to work. He shaped the head and gave it a long chin. Then he moulded a pointy nose and bulging eyes. For the hair he rolled thin strands like spaghetti.

Danny had nearly finished his head when the phone

in the hall rang. Sam and Vicki, who were both watching TV, raced to answer it.

The sounds of bodies being pushed against walls and their feet thumping on the wooden floors as they bustled for position reverberated through the house.

Sam won. The sound of Vicki's whining made Danny smile. 'That's not fair. You shouldn't push me, Sam. I'll tell Mum you pushed.'

The next voice Danny heard was Sam's. 'Muuum,' he called down the passageway. 'It's for you.'

Danny's mother wiped her hands on a tea towel. 'Who is it?'

Sam walked into the kitchen. 'It's the guy from the bank.'

Danny caught the tea towel that his mother threw across the table. Her lips tightened around clenched teeth as she muttered something angrily under her breath. She made her hand into a fist and thumped her mountain of dough. She marched out of the kitchen.

Sam walked over to Danny. 'What are you doing?'

Danny showed his little head proudly. The smile on its face mirrored Danny's. 'I'm making a head,' he announced. 'Mum's going to bake it and it will puff up and look weird.'

Sam looked envious. He walked toward Danny. '*I* want to make something.'

Danny turned away from him, protecting his dough head. 'This is my dough, you get your own.'

'I will,' Sam retorted. 'But I'm not making a silly head.' Danny didn't care. He liked his head.

Sam wandered over to the mountain of dough. He gazed at an impression of his mother's fist before he pulled a clump of dough into his hands.

Sam loved war games. He was always making bows and arrows with the bamboos near the big creek. Once he even made a catapult using a flexible tree branch, a hessian sack and Vicki's skipping rope. Sam tied the sack across the fork of the bent branch, making a nice little hammock. Then he would sit rocks in the small hammock, pull the branch down to breaking point then let go of the rope. Some of the rocks flew right across the big creek.

They spent hours catapulting rocks. It was spectacular when the bigger rocks hit the far bank. Clods of dry red soil exploded from the cliff face and into the air. The small avalanche was followed by a shower of fine dirt and a cloud of drifting dust. Sometimes, if the catapulted rock was large enough and hit just in the right place, large chunks of the bank broke away in slabs and tumbled to the creek bed, shattering on impact. There was a lot of jumping up and down and cheering when that happened, especially from Vicki.

Sam must have been thinking about war-like activity

as he moulded his dough. Danny didn't notice the wicked smile that lifted one side of his brother's face as Sam rolled, squeezed and patted his dough blob. He was making something better than a head. He had decided to make a missile. When Sam completed his missile he stopped. He looked at Danny, who was engrossed in his sculpturing, then back at his missile. Danny had no idea what went through his brother's mind at that time but it must've been something like, *Missile . . . Danny . . . missile* kill *Danny!*

With the dough nicely smoothed into a missile shape, complete with tail fins, he took aim and threw it. Hard!

Danny didn't see it coming. He was suddenly struck a fierce, head-wrenching blow . . . just below the left ear. *Thoop!* 'Ow!' The force of the blow threw his head back. The dough missile, now with an impression of Danny's earlobe on its nose, spun to the floor. *Ploop.*

Sam pointed and laughed. 'Ha, ha, ha, I told you I'd make something better than a head.'

Danny ground his teeth angrily. 'I'll get you for that!' he said.

Chuckling, Sam wriggled a beckoning finger. 'Come on then,' he teased. 'Come and get me.'

The chase was on. Sam ran. Danny set off after him. Around and around the table they went. Sam was finding it hard to keep on his feet he was laughing so much.

'You should've seen your face when the missile hit,' he mocked. 'Your hair flicked really hard. I bet you've got whiplash. I bet it hurt. Come on; admit it, it really hurt, didn't it?'

Danny made a sharp movement to his right; he trod on the missile and nearly fell backwards. 'Whoa!'

Only a wild wave of his arms above his head saved him.

Sam laughed louder. 'Ha, ha, ha,' he cried, buckling at the knees. 'My missile nearly killed you twice!'

Danny was furious and red-faced. He lifted his little dough head ready to throw. Sam stopped, facing him on the far side of the table. Laughing tears were rolling down his cheeks. He continued to duck and sway. Danny tried desperately to track his movements.

'No chance, Danny boy,' Sam teased. 'You can't hit a moving target.' Sam stuck his tongue out. 'Come on, hit me,' he taunted, rocking sharply from side to side. 'Come on, take a shot.'

Danny was determined. He ground his teeth and eyed his brother keenly. He drew his arm back and waited for just the right moment. Sam ducked under the table. Danny waited. He knew Sam would appear again. It was just a matter of patience. Waiting . . . waiting . . . waiting.

Then, sure enough, Sam's devious face rose cautiously above the horizon of the table like a cheeky glove puppet.

Danny's face looked like Tippy when he snarled and he hurled the dough as hard as he could. Sam flicked his head to one side. 'Nah, nah, you missed!' He felt the breeze of the smiling dough head as it flew past and . . . *clatter!* . . . struck a tower in the ancient city of stacked bowls.

Sam turned his head sharply and the boys watched in horror as the tower tumbled down. Despite Sam's desperate dive to stop them, two of the bowls exploded onto the hard kitchen floor. *Smash!*

Danny's little dough head lay among the ruins of the ancient city. The nose was flat and one of the eyes had pinged across the room.

Cringing, the boys exchanged horrified glances. There was nowhere to run and nowhere to hide.

They heard the phone slam down. *Clunk!* Then stomping footsteps pounded an angry rhythm, not the Beatles' *Love Me Do*, along the passageway. Their mother was on her way.

The boys swallowed. Uh oh!

The next few seconds were frozen in time. Their mouths hung open, they stood perfectly still and their eyes, wide with shock, rolled to the sound of footsteps.

Keen not to miss anything, Vicki appeared at the

kitchen door. Danny caught a glimpse of her horrified expression as she saw the evidence shattered in a thousand pieces on the kitchen floor. Vicki quickly moved to one side as her mother neared.

Danny's mother stopped at the doorway. 'What happened?' she screamed. 'Who did this?' She looked to the sink and saw Danny's small dough head.

She glared at Danny, took a step forward and grabbed his arm. 'Are you deaf? Answer me!'

Danny was startled by the ferociousness in his

mother's voice and the firmness in her grip. She was never this angry, ever.

He looked at her free hand, the one that had been kneading the dough so gently only a few minutes before. The same one that held the telephone and listened in disbelief at what the bank had to say.

Danny didn't understand how such a gentle hand had bunched suddenly into a tight, white-knuckled fist. He hadn't heard her growling angrily into the phone. The eyes he had only ever seen sparkle with gentleness now glistened with anger.

She wrenched him wildly. 'Are you stupid? You know you don't play games in the kitchen!' She pointed in the direction of the mess. 'Look what you've done! *Look!*'

Danny wanted to say that it was just a couple of bowls, that's all, just two bowls, but he was too afraid to say anything.

She slapped the kitchen bench. Danny jumped. 'You don't think! Do you?'

Tears welled in Danny's eyes. The lump in his throat choked him. His lips quivered and so did Vicki's. Their mum suddenly stopped. She looked at Vicki, then to Sam, who had taken a step back, and to Danny again. There was a strange silence. She took some deep breaths. She let her hands drop limply to her sides. Her eyelashes fluttered. Her eyebrows twitched and her lips moved but she said nothing. She had changed suddenly. The untamed wildness in her face crumbled away. Her shoulders dropped and she folded to her knees to look into Danny's eyes.

'I'm sorry, Danny,' she said.

When she moved to place her hands on his shoulders, gently this time, Danny pulled violently away. He turned and ran before the tears could roll all the way down his cheeks.

Breaking the silence he shouted, 'It's not fair! Sam started it!' He pointed at his mum. 'I hate you!' he yelled and he flew from the kitchen into the shadows of the passageway.

He turned back as he pulled the front door open. He looked down the passageway at the lonely figure of his mother standing in the kitchen doorway. 'I'm going and I'm never coming back!' he bellowed at her. 'Never! Ever!'

Danny slammed the door so hard – *bang!* – that the windows rattled.

He leapt from the verandah and moved threateningly at the chickens, kicking and stomping. They scattered noisily. Sniffling, he stopped for a second, scanned the yard and called for Tippy. 'Tippy! Tippy! Where are you? Come on, boy!'

But Tippy didn't come. He wasn't home. He was over visiting Mark Thompson.

Danny couldn't wait. Feeling completely abandoned, he ran off.

He ran across the road, past the Mundowie Institute Hall, ignoring the white soldier statue standing guard, and off to the big creek. There was only one place for him to go: his secret place. The place he had discovered only a few weeks before after Sam and Mark were mean to him. They had been racing their bikes up and down the banks of the creek in a pedal-power motorcross, Sam had called it. They had made a great track that twisted and turned through the creek bed and up and down some of the banks. But Danny found it hard to keep up in the races so they said he couldn't join in.

'You're too slow,' Mark grumbled. 'You just get in the way.'

Danny was deeply hurt when Sam agreed. 'Yeah, go home.'

Danny had thrown his bike to the ground and sulked away. He wandered along the banks of the creek throwing stones and kicking dirt. When looking up at some nests in a tree he stumbled over a branch that lay hidden in the grass. He fell flat on his face.

'Oomph!' While on the ground he peered through the grass and had an ant's-eye view of things.

Ahead of him was a huge old tree, rotten and decaying. At the base he spied a hole big enough for him to squeeze through. Curious, he cautiously poked his head in to take a peek. He found the tree was burnt out and hollow. He squirmed all the way in and managed to stand. It was like a tiny cave. The top of the tree was crumbling, allowing fine fingers of sunlight to spear into the shadowy place. Danny imagined they were spotlights for performing ants. Spider webs wrapped his face and bugs crawled along his arms. After brushing them away madly Danny had decided then and there that he would clean this tree cave out and create his secret crypt.

That was where he would live from now on: no brothers, no sisters and no mums!

He marched to the edge of the creek, kicking stones. He was wearing his old sneakers with the holes in the toes. He could hear his mother's voice in his head. *Don't forget to wear your boots. There are snakes about.* Danny kicked the ground hard and made a dust cloud. 'What do you care, Mum?' he sniffled.

At a narrow section of the creek Danny went to a gum tree on the very edge of the bank. The spot was a long way down from where he and Sam normally crossed. His hide-out was on the other side. Danny had a rope tied to an overhanging branch. He could swing like a monkey from one side to the other.

The first time he'd tried swinging he wasn't too successful. He hadn't bothered measuring the rope. It was too long and he went crashing, head first, into the opposite bank. There was a lump on his head the size of a golf ball and the cut on his knee made blood maps on his jeans. Danny didn't give up; he soon got it right and hadn't had any problems since.

He loved to swing through the air. Danny thought it was as close to flying as he could get. The wind would push through his hair and he could look down into the creek far below at the huge fallen trees, boulders and cliff faces. The feeling of adventure was one that seemed to belong far away in bigger, more important places than Mundowie, places like the Grand Canyon that he'd seen on the TV. Mundowie would never be on TV.

As soon as he was under his swinging tree Danny took the rope in his hands. There was a huge knot at the end upon which he could put his feet. Wrapping the rope around his hands he took a few steps back, hung on and ran off the edge of the creek.

'Yahoooo!'

The branch above creaked as Danny became airborne. Away he flew, spinning. The breeze cooled his face as he looked down into the creek bed. There were weeds, stones and a tangle of rusty barbed wire. The flight across the creek was even more exciting when the heavy rains came and wild water rapids surged below. Debris then included logs, pieces of iron and old doors sailing beneath him at great speed. The wild currents then were like giant veins and the water was the colour of gravy.

But not today, the creek was dusty dry. The smell of dust filled Danny's nostrils as he landed, skidding, safely on the other side. Some interested sheep stopped what they were doing and watched him tie his rope to a fallen tree. He would need it for the return journey.

He wiped his dribbling nose with his sleeve, leaving a silver trail, then he walked the narrow grassy track to his secret tree. It was bare. There was only the trunk and one branch remaining on the grey skeleton. Danny dropped to his knees and began to crawl in through the hole at the base – the entrance was hard to see because Danny kept it camouflaged with leaves and grass. He squirmed into the shadowy sanctuary of his secret place. The sheep stood and watched with interest as his wriggling bum disappeared.

Inside his small tree cave he kept all the treasures he collected around the farm. Things like snakeskins and sheep skulls.

The sheep skull was a real prize. It had belonged to a ram. The curling horns and dirty teeth were awesome. He had used the skull once to scare Vicki. He had sat it in the grimy tractor-shed window one dark night and placed a candle inside. When the candle was lit the rotten teeth and the eye sockets glowed with an eerie yellow light. It was brilliant!

He couldn't let such a good thing go to waste and so, standing outside the back door, he had called Vicki out into the velvet darkness. 'Hey Vicki! Come out here for a minute.'

She came skipping happily outside. 'Yeah, what do you want?'

Danny pointed to his unearthly creation. 'Look.'

Vicki launched herself into the air. 'Aagggghhhhh!' She covered her eyes and ran back into the house. 'Agggghhhh!' Through the kitchen. 'Aghhhhhh!' And up the passageway. 'Aghhhhhh!' She didn't stop screaming until she found their mum trying to watch the news.

Apparently, poor Vicki still had nightmares about the glowing sheep's head. It was pretty good though. Even Sam had been scared.

The sheep's skull had a decaying snakeskin lying beside it and was staring up at Danny as he crawled inside the trunk. Danny thought of Vicki and wondered what she was doing. She hadn't been mean to him; he still liked Vicki. Maybe she was out looking for him . . . but no, not if there was a feast on.

'I bet they're all sitting in the kitchen laughing now,' he thought. 'Laughing and having the feast without me.'

Danny sighed as he realised he might be missing out

on the feast. Food was one thing he hadn't thought about. There was nothing to eat in his secret place. Danny shook himself as he stood. Feast or not, it didn't matter; he wasn't going back, no way.

Fingers of sunlight with floating specks of dust drifting around within them poked through from above, offering enough light to take away complete blackness. There wasn't a lot of room. Danny could stand in the middle and easily touch both sides.

Danny looked down as he waited for his eyes to adjust. A shaft of sunlight shone on his sneakers. Danny's toe was sticking out. He gave it a wriggle.

Danny heard a sound on his left, where the sheep skull sat in a bed of dead leaves. The sound was soft like a whisper. *Shhhhh.*

Danny froze. He stared at the spot. Behind the skull there was a small hole to the outside world. The leaves around the hole were moving. *Shhhhh.*

Rolling his eyes he listened to be sure he wasn't hearing things. Danny heard it again, the sound of something moving. *Shhhhh.*

He blinked his eyes furiously and although he didn't see anything, he knew what it was. A snake!

His heart pounded and his breathing quickened. Danny dared not move. Like his sinister visitor, he was cornered.

Nothing likes to be cornered.

Danny's quivering lips were suddenly dry. He swallowed nervously, eyes still staring hard.

Shhhhh. There was more movement, this time slow and sneaky, as though searching for something. Searching for Danny?

Danny backed up against the crusty wall of the old tree. He pushed back hard and froze as if standing on a very narrow ledge outside the window of a skyscraper. He spread his fingers across the roughness of the decaying tree. His eyes darted left, right, left, right.

Where is it? Where is it? he thought.

Time slowed. A single second dragged.

With wide eyes, Danny listened intently and tracked the soft sounds. *Shhhh . . . crackle.*

Then, he saw something through the shadows behind the ram's skull. It looked cold, round and beautifully brown. He stared hard.

He didn't see the head or the tail, just the fattest part of the curling body as it slithered through the eye socket of the skull and moved slowly beneath one of the sunbeams. The sunlight shone on the snake highlighting the glistening skin. It was moving slowly and as far as Danny could tell it didn't know yet that he was there. He glanced down at his twisted shorts and his exposed legs. If only he were wearing his boots.

Something crawled down his neck. A beetle? Cockroach? Ant? Spider! The crawling thing moved into his shirt and across his shoulders, exploring. Danny flinched. His feet shuffled. He couldn't help it.

Mistake! His sharp movement startled the snake.

With a whip of its body, its tail darted from the eye socket of the skull and it turned to Danny with its tongue flicking menacingly.

Feeling threatened, the snake lifted its head instinctively, ready to strike. Its head hovered in a sunbeam like a marionette on an invisible string. It was so close, with wicked eyes and a wicked tongue ready to fight.

Danny had never been face to face with a snake. He'd seen plenty by the tractor shed, in the chicken yard and near the creek, but had never been close enough to eyeball one. The head was small and the mouth thin. The skin, with its fine scales, was shiny, well polished for a creature that slid about in dirt. Danny stared for an instant into its piercing eyes and he shivered. This was just like a Mark Thompson snake story.

Mark was always telling scary snake stories. His recent favourite was the story of the brown snake that jumped up off the road and into the open car window of a guy driving down a gravel road near Port Bilton. In a vampire-like attack it sunk its fangs into the neck of the driver. They found him slumped over the wheel and the snake hiding under the bonnet coiled around the engine where it was nice and warm. But it got away before anyone could catch it. And to put it in Mark's words, 'Just think, that snake is still lurking out there somewhere, so beware, boys.'

And in his next breath Mark had turned to Danny and said, 'It's probably the same snake whose old skin you stole over near the Miller homestead. He'll be after you, Danny boy. I don't reckon they'd like you taking their old skins.'

Danny suddenly thought that if this *was* the leaping vampire snake out for revenge because of the stolen skin then it could easily jump at him and sink its fangs into *his* neck.

The thought of fangs sinking into his neck made Danny's breathing quicken even more. He wanted to cry out. He wanted to be home in the kitchen, feasting. He opened his mouth to call for help, but no sound would come. And even if it did, he knew no one would hear him.

He was on his own, just as he'd wanted only a few minutes before. Survival was in his hands. Escape! He had to escape! Danny's mind raced with foolish thoughts.

He eyed the small entrance. It was so close. He thought about making a dive for the door, but then he had visions of the snake sinking its fangs into his bum as he struggled on all fours to pull himself to freedom.

He knew enough to realise that if he were bitten, the farmhouse was a long way away. If he had to walk that far the poison would surge through his body. He wouldn't survive.

With his back pushed hard against the trunk of the tree Danny's squirming hands felt the roughness, the coolness of rotting wood. The creature crawling across his back moved over his shoulder, down his arm and rested on the back of his hand. It was probably a red-back spider. If the snake didn't kill him, the red-back would.

Danny's body shivered as he thought that maybe the words he had screamed at his mother in the kitchen would come true. He would never come home, ever. No one knew where he was. They would never find his body. His sad spirit would wander the fields like the headless Miller woman.

The snake kept still, as though waiting for Danny to make the first move. Its tongue tasted the air. Perhaps it could taste Danny's fear.

Danny's next passing thought was to arm himself. He looked for a stick. He looked for a stone. He looked for anything. The ram's skull caught his eye. The foolish plan he made in a split second of panic was that he would dive across, scoop up the skull and throw it. One of the horns would stab the snake.

That's how things happen in movies, he thought, *and that's how things will happen here. It isn't difficult – a quick dive and then throw.*

Before Danny could put his master plan into action the head of the snake suddenly dipped low. There was movement. *Shhhh.*

Danny closed his eyes tightly and braced himself for the needle of a fang to spike his leg or his arm. He felt nothing.

He opened his eyes again. His head flicked in all directions. *Where is it? Where's it gone?*

Terrified, Danny tried to trace the telltale sounds of movement. He looked down at his feet. He saw something brown, but couldn't tell what it was. Leaves? Bark? Or was it the snake?

Don't lift the feet. Don't tread on anything. Keep still, Dad always says. If you see a snake just keep still. Huh! That's easy to say.

Danny wanted to run, jump, kick, stamp and scream, all at once.

He gasped as the tip of the snake's moving tail touched the toe that protruded from his sneaker. He kept his eyes glued on the tail as it slid, twisting and curling, out of the entrance and away into the open sunlight.

Relieved, he slapped the crawling thing from the back of his hand. 'Get off!'

Then he suddenly found his voice. '*Heeeelp!*'

His mournful cry died in echoes. No one heard him.

Danny suddenly felt weak and floppy. He dropped to his knees, breathing hard. The flaking snakeskin that he had collected from the rocks near the old Miller homestead lay next to the sheep skull. Danny gazed at it and it set him thinking. He wondered about the snake and if it was in fact the jumping vampire snake. Danny picked up the decaying skin and it flaked away in his fingers. Flakes drifted to the ground and he thought of the broken plates in the kitchen and his mum. He wouldn't tell her about the snake; she might yell at him for not wearing his boots. He decided he would go, but not yet.

He spent the afternoon wandering the big creek. Every snap of a twig, every crunch of rolling stone beneath his feet made him jump.

He devised an alarm system for his hide-out. He put a large flat rock by the entrance to use every time he visited. His plan was to throw it inside and see if anything came scurrying out. Once it was all clear he would crawl inside. He also decided to bring a torch with him the next time he ran away from home.

Late in the afternoon, when his hide-out was in complete shadow, Danny swung back across the creek and sauntered back to Mundowie. He was hungry and tired and was sure his mum had learnt her lesson.

He stopped under the lengthening shadow of the Mundowie Hall. He sat at the feet of the soldier statue to think for a minute. It was here that he decided he would tell his mum just how unfair she'd been and if she did it again he wouldn't come back next time.

As Danny sat, he was disturbed by a sound in the grass at the side of the hall. Danny spun round. The dry grass was long – and it moved!

Something was shuffling through it, creeping up on him. Given Mark's story about the snake hunting him for revenge, Danny jumped to the obvious conclusion.

He sprung to his feet with no time to think. It didn't really matter what he said to his mum. Just as long as he was safe at home and hadn't missed out on the entire feast. He wasn't hanging around this time to let the snake tickle his toes with its tail. He took off!

When he started running he couldn't resist taking a glance back over his shoulder. What he saw made him slow to a casual jog. There was no reason for him to be afraid. He shook his head and laughed when he saw what emerged from the long grass. Tippy bounded into view with his tail spinning. He called to Danny. *Yap, yap.* Tippy had been searching the town for him.

Then he scooted out of the shadows of the hall and set off after Danny. Danny skidded to a stop and squatted to greet his little pal.

'Hey! Tippy boy.' Danny ruffled Tippy's ears playfully. 'Where have you been?'

They trotted off side by side as usual. They spun and jumped together all the way home.

When he crept into the kitchen Danny's mum and dad were there. They were both sitting at the table, their heads in their hands. They didn't see him walk in; they had their backs to the door and were fumbling through a blizzard of papers that lay spread across the table. They were both hanging over the table like broken branches hanging from dying trees at the creek. The word *BANK* was written in large black letters down the spines of the three thick folders that lay stacked on the floor. It was his dad's writing.

On the kitchen cupboard, Danny spied two freshly baked biscuits sprinkled with hundreds and thousands and a cupcake smothered in pink icing sitting on a plate next to a fresh loaf of bread. There was a small piece of coloured paper next to the plate. It was a note and the note read: *Danny's feast – don't touch.* It was Vicki's writing. She'd also drawn a happy face.

Danny stepped in quietly with one eye on his parents and one on his plate of cakes. His parents were talking softly in serious tones. Danny watched as his mother put her arm across his dad's back and rested her head on his shoulder.

Danny's dad shook his head and sighed heavily. 'I'm sorry,' he breathed. 'I can't see a way out.'

When Danny lifted his plate, Vicki's note drifted toward the floor like a feather.

Danny's parents saw it land. Surprised, they both snapped to attention and looked up.

Danny looked nervously across the open space.

'Danny boy,' his dad said brightly.

His mum looked to his feet. She smiled. 'You aren't wearing your boots,' she said softly.

Danny wanted to go to her, but his pride held him back.

'I didn't see any snakes anyway,' he lied, and he walked up the passageway to his bedroom to eat.

When Danny went to his bed he found a small parcel wrapped in coloured tissue paper sitting on his pillow. He was curious. He put his feast on his bed and picked up the parcel.

There was a note. It said simply, *For my Danny boy*.

Danny knew it was his mother's writing. He clawed at the coloured paper to reveal his present. There, gazing up at him, smiling crookedly, was a well-baked head.

He smiled, and then his smile rumbled into a throaty chuckle. He threw the paper to the floor and rested the crusty, bread-dough head in the palm of his hand.

The hair had swollen and the nose was all bent. The eyes popped and the expression on the face was hilarious. Danny turned it this way and that.

He continued to chuckle until he heard the bedroom door open.

His mum walked in. 'What do you think?' she asked.

'Brilliant.' Danny beamed. 'Look at the hair . . . and the nose.'

His mother walked toward him until she was so close Danny could smell baked cakes, bread and biscuits. Danny took a deep breath. Ahhhh! There was nothing better than the smell of warm cakes, biscuits or freshly baked bread . . . except maybe the smell of rain on a really hot day . . . or the smell of freshly cut wheat when his dad was harvesting.

Still amazed by his baked head, Danny's delight overcame his pride and he leant into his mum's warm and safe embrace. He buried his head in her flour-dusted apron and she ruffled his hair.

Danny didn't say anything about his adventure. After all, he might never see that snake again.

'Now off to bed,' she whispered, kissing the top of his head. 'And tomorrow, don't forget to wear your boots, please. There are snakes about.'

He smiled up at her sheepishly. 'I will, Mum, don't worry.'

5
Tippy

Danny's mother opened the screen door. It squealed like a kitten whose tail had been caught in the hinges. She walked out onto the verandah.

The old blue tractor was bouncing along the crest of a small hill near the creek. Danny and Sam were riding the tractor with their dad. She smiled when she heard the echo of their laughter.

Danny, who had made sure to slip his boots on that morning, was sitting next to his father, clinging to the mudguard. The old tractor wasn't fast, just bouncy. Sam was standing on a small platform behind the seat with his hands on his father's shoulders. He looked like the captain of an old sailing ship standing on deck for a voyage of great discovery.

Tippy was running beside them barking madly, stopping occasionally to sniff and cock his leg. Danny called to him constantly. 'Keep up, Tippy! Come on, boy! Come on!'

Danny spied his mum and waved to her as the tractor growled along. 'Helloooo Muuuum!' he bellowed.

She waved back with exaggerated sweeping movements of her arms above her head. Danny thought she looked like a person stranded on a desert island waving to her rescuers. Danny kept his eye on her until the tractor dipped into a gully and out of sight.

A trail of drifting dust mapped its journey. Danny's mum bowed her head, turned away and walked inside.

She heard singing coming from her bedroom. *Tra, la, la, la, la, dee, dah*. She crept along the passageway and, stopping at the door, spied Vicki dancing in front of the mirror. She was wearing her mum's finest jewellery. Smiling to herself, Danny's mum waltzed in to sing with her.

The tractor rumbled down a gentle slope. Sam leant forward and pointed like any sea captain on a voyage of discovery would. 'Head for those bumps, Dad. They'll *really* make her bounce.'

Danny saw the bumps and smiled expectantly up at his dad. 'Yeah, go on, Dad.'

His dad gave him a wink. He was wearing his favourite hat, the one with an oil stain at the front that looked like a tiny map of Africa. He took a hand quickly from the wheel and pushed his hat firmly onto his head. 'You hang on tightly then, boys!' he cried playfully. He steered toward the bumps, but eased off on the speed – safe and sure.

They hit the small landscape of bumps with a childish cry from their dad. 'Whahoo!' Sam wrapped his arms around his dad's neck.

Despite the lack of speed, the bouncing was wicked! Unseen parts of the tractor rattled and clanked. The mudguard creaked and shuddered. Danny's knuckles were white with the firmness of his grip. Danny's dad threw a glance at him. 'Hang on to that mudguard Danny. The old girl might fall to bits.'

'Ha, ha, ha, I've got it, Dad. She'll be all right!'

The boys laughed. And the more they laughed, the harder it was to keep a firm grip.

Danny's dad patted the body of the tractor as if it were a tame beast. 'Good on you, old girl. Keep going.'

Some farmers had huge tractors with cabins, air conditioners and soft seats. But not Danny Allen's dad.

He kept saying he was going to buy a decent machine just as soon as he had a good year. He'd been saying that for ages. There hadn't been a good year for a while, so they were stuck with the old rattler.

Danny didn't care. He loved the old thing. You couldn't have a wild tractor ride, he thought, in a cabin with air conditioning and soft seats.

Danny leant over and peered down at the huge black tyre spinning beneath him. The thick teeth of the tread were biting ferociously into the dry earth.

Tippy was running along happily, clever enough to keep a safe distance. Every now and then, when the grass was too long for his short legs, he would spring into the air. If he looked like slowing, Danny would urge him on.

'Come on, Tippy! Come on, boy!'

The little dog always responded with a yap and an impressive burst of speed. Danny was marvelling at Tippy's acceleration when they hit a pothole camouflaged by a thatch of dry grass. The boys were momentarily airborne. 'Whoa!'

Danny's dad had to straighten his hat. Surprised by the jolt, he slowed down.

'Go faster, Dad!' Danny cried. 'That was unreal!'

Danny's father raised a hand. 'No, that's fast enough,' he called. 'Tractors can roll easily, always remember that.'

Every time he had the chance Danny's dad would tell the boys things about tractors, or crops, or sheep. Danny wanted to remember everything his dad told him because he figured that he and Sam would run the farm one day.

Danny liked the idea of being a farmer. He liked the idea of being just like his dad. He would need a dusty hat with oil stains though.

Down a small gully and up the other side they rumbled. The tractor riders weren't only out to have fun; they had a job to do. A section of the fence that ran along the highest bank of the creek was down. They were soon riding through long grass beneath the flickering shade of crowded trees. Sam pointed and cried, 'There it is, Dad, just ahead.'

'Thanks son, I see it.'

Danny saw it as well. A large section of the bank had been undermined and had crumbled away, taking fence posts and wire with it. Some of the older posts lay splintered in the creek bed below.

The concern was that without the fence some of the sheep might wander too close to the edge and parts of the bank were unstable and could give way at any time.

Danny felt that some of the sheep were already standing too close. When Danny set eyes on them he immediately thought of Vicki and smiled. The day before, when the three children were sitting on the front verandah watching Tippy bully the chickens as he hunted for stale crusts that had just been scattered for them, Vicki had asked Sam why the fence needed fixing.

Sam gave her a silly answer. He was a good storyteller. He didn't grin or smirk once.

'If Dad doesn't fix that fence, it will be awful,' he explained very seriously. 'Our sheep could be in *terrible* danger. You must have heard them bleating loudly sometimes.'

Vicki sat, mouth open, peering intently up at her big brother. 'Yep, I have,' she said keenly.

'Yeah, well that's it,' said Sam. 'That's the sound they make when they try to fly.' He made his hands flutter like little wings above Vicki's head. Her eyes widened as she watched them. Sam leant forward and said, 'If one tries to fly over the creek then the rest will follow. That's what sheep are like. Most of them can't think for themselves; they just follow each other. So they'll all line up and jump.'

Vicki looked shocked. Sam knew he had her. 'They'll flap their legs madly,' he continued enthusiastically, 'but they won't get far. Over the edge and down they'll go . . .' Sam made a diving motion with his hands. 'Then . . . *splat!*' He slapped his hands loudly on the verandah.

Vicki jumped.

Sam leant in close to her and made a sickly face. 'We could have a pile of dead flying sheep, all squished with blood and guts, on the creek bed.'

Vicki recoiled. 'Yuck!'

Sam's flying sheep story was the reason Vicki didn't want to travel on the tractor that morning. She was afraid of finding a pile of dead sheep in the creek, or being a witness to some bone-crunching, gut-splattering crash landings.

When the boys left her she was drawing chalk pictures on the cracked path near the verandah. She was obviously still thinking about the sheep. When the boys walked past, she stopped drawing and said, 'I've got an idea. I think the sheep should wear parachutes.' She pointed to her pictures. 'See?' she beamed proudly. She'd drawn a flock of little sheep parachuting through white fluffy clouds. 'That will save them and they will still get to fly . . . sort of.'

The boys had walked off, sniggering.

When the tractor slowed with a loud squeal Danny gazed at the sheep gathered under a nearby tree. He imagined them all lining up, like paratroopers in a plane, ready to jump off the cliff. He chuckled at the thought of parachuting sheep.

Danny's dad brought the tractor to a jerking halt. The creek was wide at this point. This was one of

Danny's favourite spots. It was where the billabong formed after the rains.

There was an old tyre tied to a rope that hung from one of the branches reaching out over the cliff's edge. When the billabong was full, Danny, Sam and Mark Thompson loved to swing out and drop into the deepest water.

At the top of the high cliff, overlooking the creek, sat three old rusty drums. The drums had been used for lots of things. They had once been part of a raft that the boys made. Danny would never forget it; there had been rain and the creek was running.

It had been Mark Thompson's idea. 'We'll tie the drums together with rope and sail it downstream. We might get to parts of the creek we've never seen before. It will be like a voyage into the unknown.'

They had rolled the drums to a bank at a deep part of the creek where the water was flowing quickly. The bank was wet and sloped perfectly so that when the raft was finished they could slide it into the water. 'That's how they launch real ships,' Mark had said expertly. 'They hit the bow with a bottle of champagne and slide them down big ramps.' Danny was impressed by Mark's knowledge of ship launching.

They worked for a whole afternoon tying the drums together with ropes. The drum raft had an old door as its deck that they had carried down from the tractor shed. It had a stick for a mast and a torn wheat bag for a sail.

When they were ready to launch they found a rotten, white ant-ridden post and pretended it was a bottle of champagne. They shattered it on one of the drums. White ants fizzed from the post like the froth from a champagne bottle. Mark stood on deck as self-appointed captain while Danny and Sam pushed the raft down the slippery slope.

Mark shouted instructions above the roar of the water. 'Push harder, you guys! Make it slide fast and when it hits the water, jump on!'

But when the raft gurgled into the water Sam and Danny had no hope of scrambling aboard. They fell flat on their faces!

The wild water was so fast it pulled the raft into the hungry veins of the twisting current. The raft spun and bobbed. Mark Thompson looked worried.

'Hey!' he screamed. 'You guys! What are you doing? Get out here!'

Danny and Sam watched helplessly as Mark sailed out of reach.

He was setting off on a voyage to the unknown, alone! 'Help meeee!'

Sam and Danny ran along the bank trying to keep up. Mark was spinning and bobbing, yelling and screaming. 'I'm going to drown!'

'Swim for it!' Sam yelled.

'I can't.'

'Why not?'

'I can't swim!'

Danny was stunned. Mark Thompson couldn't swim?

Mark wrapped his arms and legs around the flimsy mast and clung to it like a koala up a tree. 'Get a rope! Get something! Help me!'

Before Sam and Danny could react to his instructions, Mark spiralled into a whirlpool of rapids. 'I'm going to be sick!' The raft then spun into a huge floating log. *Crunch!* And like a ship thrown onto a reef, it quickly broke apart.

Obviously terrified – his face said it all – Mark looked at the boys and screamed, 'I'm going under!'

Somehow, when the mast toppled, Mark lunged at one of the bobbing drums and clung to it. He sailed along, yelling and screaming, until his drum ran aground. Relieved that his feet could touch the bottom, he scrambled through shallow water to the bank. He was shivering and coughing when Danny and Sam pulled him to his feet. Mark's teeth were chattering loudly when he looked at Sam and Danny and blamed them for the shipwreck. 'Next time *I'll* tie all of the ropes,' he grumbled. 'You guys are useless!'

But there had never been a next time. When the creek dried out the boys found the drums and rolled them to the top of the bank, where they became seats for spectators.

Sam called them 'the grandstand'.

When someone was swinging out across the calm water of the billabong ready to drop from the tyre and do a bomb, the others would sit on the drums and watch. They had scorecards and if you did a good bomb they would hold up a ten.

Danny had only got a ten once. Sam had pushed him out across the water when he wasn't ready. He lost his grip on the rope and had fallen with his arms waving wildly and his legs kicking frantically. Spinning like a human frisbee, he screamed all the way down. 'Aggghhhhhhhhhhhhhhh!' Then . . . *smack*!

He hit the water, back first.

He came up spluttering and coughing. He was going to yell at Sam, but when he heard Mark Thompson cheering and saw him holding up a ten, Danny was rapt.

Standing at the edge of the creek, seeing the tyre dangling on the rope and the drums sitting in a line, reminded Danny of his perfect score of ten.

He smiled and called to his brother. 'Hey Sam, remember . . .'

Sam turned his back and started walking away. 'Yeah I know, you got a ten from Thommo when you did that bomb.'

Danny beamed. 'You remember it, then?'

'You won't let me forget it! You mention it every time we come here.'

Sam waddled off to sit on a drum. There was a stone in his boot. He walked funny.

Danny's dad was pulling at a rotting post. The wood crumbled in his fingers and a writhing mass of white ants was sent into a blur of panic. He danced around them. Some of them ran over his hands. He flicked them away and kicked the post. An explosion of dust, grit and splinters flew to the air.

Tippy barked.

Danny's dad jumped back. He brushed his sleeves feverishly and tugged at his shirt.

'What is it, Dad?' Danny asked.

'I saw a spider,' his father replied. He spun about brushing himself madly. 'I hate spiders running over me.'

Danny was surprised. He didn't think his dad was afraid of anything.

'It's going up your leg, Dad!' Danny cried.

Danny's father did a little jump and shook his leg violently.

Danny pointed and laughed. 'Just kidding.'

His father pushed his hat from his brow and glared. 'That's not funny, Danny.'

Danny disagreed. It was hilarious.

Tippy picked up a piece of the crumbling post and

dropped it at Danny's feet. He stood back, panting and eyeing his new stick, waiting for Danny to throw it. He obliged. Picking it up, he made it spin like a boomerang. Tippy took off, ears pinned back, tiny muscle-bound legs a blur. He darted through the dry grass.

Danny stared at him, watched his every dodge and weave. With an overzealous skid he scooped the stick into his mouth and came trotting proudly back. The stick was returned again and again.

Danny was happily playing with Tippy when, out of the corner of his eye, he suddenly sensed his father moving slowly toward the drums. Puzzled, Danny watched him.

His dad pulled at his hat and craned his neck. His brow furrowed and his gaze was intense.

Danny tracked his father's gaze to Sam, who was still sitting on the drum. He had one shoe off and was looking down as if he'd dropped something. Danny heard a soft rumble from within the drum. So did Sam.

He froze.

◆

'Don't move, Sam!' their father called, as he quickened his approach.

Sam sat staring curiously at the drum beneath him.
'Why not?'

Then they all heard the sound again – shuffling
and writhing. There was a rusty hole at the base of
the drum. Sam's weight had been enough to push the
drum down and block the hole.

Their dad broke into a gallop. He pointed sternly at
Sam. 'Stay on the drum!'

Sam's fingers clutched at the drum. He glanced
uncertainly from his father to the drum and back to his
father again.

Danny stood, mesmerised. The fear he had felt in his hide-out the day he'd run away from home came flooding back. Goosebumps prickled across his shoulders and down his spine.

Danny's father raised a flat hand at Sam. 'Just keep still, son!' he urged. 'Okay?'

Sam could see the concern in his father's eyes. 'What, Dad?' he said. 'What is it?'

'Just do what I tell you. Stay on the drum.'

Danny moved forward to run with his father. Danny's dad grabbed him and with a grasp as fierce as Danny had ever felt from his father he was thrown backwards.

'You stay right where you are.'

'But what's wrong, Dad?'

'I said, stay there!'

'Why?'

'There's a snake under the drum!'

'A snake!'

Sam's eyes darted frantically, searching the base of the drum. 'Help me, Dad.'

'I'm coming. Don't move.'

Danny stood transfixed. The warm breeze brushed his terrified face and made his wide-open eyes water. His father approached the drum. Sam reached for him and moved to jump.

'No!' his father snapped. 'Don't stand!'

Danny looked at Sam and wished he were there

with his brother. When Tippy came and dropped his stick at Danny's feet, Danny ignored him.

Sam suddenly screamed. 'I'm getting off, Dad!'

Sam didn't wait for his father's response. He pushed himself from his perch only to lose his footing and stumble to the ground, his frantic feet kicking up dust. Onto his knees he fell. His hands were clawing clumsily at the ground and his feet – one of them without a shoe – kicked desperately. Danny mirrored the terrified look on his brother's face.

Danny's dad lunged at Sam and grabbed him. He flung Sam out of harm's way with his strong arms.

Sam scrambled to his feet.

Their dad quickly kicked the drum as hard as he could. It spun through the air and rolled away. Over the edge of the cliff it went, rumbling and banging into the creek. Every cockatoo for miles around seemed to take flight.

Danny stood looking through the cloud of dust drifting around his father. It was like watching a dream. Then Danny yelled, 'Snake, Dad! Look out!'

Danny's dad lost his footing on a stone and fell onto his back. He sat up quickly and froze. His hat was on the ground, upside down, the Africa stain unseen.

He had always told the boys that when they saw a snake all they had to do was keep still. *Do that and it will go on its way.*

He did just that. He sat perfectly still.

Danny was in awe of his father's bravery. He was convinced it was the leaping vampire snake set to defend itself, just as it had been when in Danny's tree. It was afraid too.

A second of stillness and uncertainty increased the tension. So much so that Sam panicked. He thought the snake was too close to his dad. He couldn't stand back and watch. He picked up a long branch and charged like a knight wielding a sword.

Danny couldn't believe it. They'd always been taught *never* to approach a snake. 'Stop, Sam!' Danny cried, grabbing at his brother's arm. '*Dooooon't!*'

Sam pulled away and charged. Danny's father screamed at him. 'Get back, Sam!'

Sam would not retreat. He swung awkwardly at the snake with his weapon. He missed and struck the ground with the impact of a small exploding bomb.

Clods of earth flew into the air. The snake whipped itself round. With speed impossible to see, it flew at Danny's father, who pulled his legs back. Incredibly, the snake missed. Sam sliced the air again with his pathetic weapon.

The snake turned to him. Sam was clumsily fumbling with his branch like a soldier in battle trying to reload his gun. Something sharp pricked the foot without a shoe. He was off balance.

The snake turned to its attacker, ready to strike. At the height it was hovering, its fangs would sink into the top of Sam's thigh, perhaps even the groin — a deadly strike. Danny's father was on his backside on the ground. Danny's heart sank when he realised there was nothing he or his dad could do.

Suddenly, the startling blur of a small black and white figure snarled from the shadows and dashed through the dust. Danny stared in disbelief.

'Noooo!' he hollered. 'Tiiiippppy! Noooo!'

The small dog leapt ferociously into battle. Danny's

dad dragged himself away and rose to his feet. Sam didn't dare attack for fear of hitting Tippy.

Danny's dad reached out to Sam. 'Give me that stick,' he growled loudly. 'And get back to Danny.'

Tippy stood barking incessantly.

Danny's dad called desperately to Tippy. 'Leave it, Tippy! Leave it, boy! *Leave it!*'

Tippy would not pull back. He was growling and snarling, daring the snake to take up the challenge.

Tippy circled and the snake, still poised to strike, tracked his movements. Tippy crouched, just as he did when waiting for Danny to throw his stick. He showed his teeth in a snarl, ready to pounce.

'Tippy!' Danny hollered, thumping his fists desperately to his knees. 'Tippy! Come here! Now!'

Tippy had never been very obedient.

There was a flash of movement and dust rose above the fierce tangle of the frenzied fighters. Danny watched in horror. Tippy's snarling head was shaking and whipping. His body, twisting and jumping, was a blur lost in a tiny tornado. Amid the snarling came a shrill yelp that pierced Danny's heart.

Tippy did not give up the fight. He flew snapping at the snake. He took it in his jaws and tossed his head violently. The snake's body was a blur in the dust. Tippy shook it violently again and again and again.

All the while, three desperate voices called to him.

'Tippy! No! Leave it! Come here, boy! Come now!'

But the fierce little dog wasn't letting go. Not until he was sure he'd won. He growled and snarled determinedly.

In the terrible minutes that followed, Tippy's wild movements slowed.

The snake too, with its torn flesh, was weak. Once he knew he was safe, Danny's dad moved in to finish it off. Tippy was staggering. Danny ran to him. Danny's dad took the snake and tossed it, spinning, into the creek.

Danny scooped up the little dog into his arms. 'Good boy, Tippy, you're all right. You'll be all right now.' Danny looked to his dad for reassurance. 'Won't he, Dad?'

Tippy was panting hard. He wagged his tail and smiled. His coat was dusty and speckled with the splash of brilliant red blood.

Danny tried to wipe some of it away with his hands. A shadow loomed over him. Danny's dad squatted beside Danny. 'He's a little hero, that dog,' he said, ruffling Tippy's ears.

'He'll be all right, won't he, Dad?' asked Danny desperately.

Danny's dad didn't answer as quickly as Danny was hoping he might. Danny's face buckled. 'Won't he?' he pleaded.

Danny's dad gently stroked Tippy's head with his rough hands. 'I don't know,' he said. 'I can't see where the snake got him.'

'How do you know he got him at all?' asked Sam hopefully. 'He might have missed.'

'Yeah,' chirped Danny. 'He's just tired after the fight.' Danny pushed his cheek next to Tippy's snout.

Danny's dad looked into Tippy's eyes. 'Hold him and keep him as still as you can, Danny,' he said quickly. 'Let's get him home, then we can take him to Port Bilton. The vet will know what to do.'

Danny's dad drove the tractor back to the house faster than he should have. Danny nursed Tippy, who began panting harder and faster, all the way home. And all the way to Port Bilton Danny talked to Tippy, saying things like: 'When the vet fixes you we'll take you home and you can rest. Mum will give you cakes and biscuits. Tomorrow I'll throw more sticks for you and you can come over to the hall and watch me climb the lookout tree. You can pee on the soldier's foot. We can even chase chickens if you like. You little bully!'

Tippy's response became less and less natural. Danny was as afraid as Tippy.

When they charged into the veterinary clinic the little dog was hanging on by a thread. The vet quickly examined the now-unconscious Tippy and shook his head. 'I'm sorry, Danny, I can't help him.'

'Can't you just give him an injection to make him better?' Danny said. 'Do something, anything, please!'

The vet shook his head again.

Tippy died under the gentle stroke of Danny's hand and the sorrowful sound of his inconsolable weeping.

That night Danny couldn't sleep for the redness of his eyes and the hurt inside that was so bad he felt it would never go away. Images of Tippy scattering chickens, begging for food, running with the tractor, chasing a stick and peeing on the soldier statue's foot in front of the Mundowie Institute Hall kept appearing. As he tossed and turned they wouldn't leave him. If only tomorrow could be yesterday and all the memories would be real again. If only the warm patch at the end of his bed were there.

Danny held his pillow and lay awake listening to Vicki sobbing and his mother singing softly to her. *Tra, la, la, la, la, dee, dah.* Across the room he heard Sam snuffling.

Late into the night light from the tractor shed filtered in through his window. The tractor had started clunking noisily on the way back from the creek. Danny had begged his dad not to stop, so he hadn't. And now he was hard at work trying to fix whatever had gone wrong. He would need the tractor the next day. The fence by the creek still hadn't been mended.

Danny spent the following day wandering aimlessly. He climbed his lookout tree and sat on his branch dangling his legs. In the afternoon he stood by the creek throwing sticks like boomerangs, but they never came back.

Later in the week, he took Tippy's collar from under his pillow and went to the creek to put it in his secret place with the other treasures. This time, he remembered to wear his boots.

Just over a week after Tippy died, on a Friday evening just before sunset, Danny's dad arrived in the truck with Mr Thompson. Danny was sitting on the front step. He was throwing little sticks and stones at the chickens to make them scatter.

His dad climbed from the truck and came walking through the gate. There was something moving under his arm, hidden under his hat. Danny's dad wasn't much good at wrapping presents. Mind you, this one would have been impossible to wrap.

Danny took little notice until his dad called him. 'Danny, come and help me, please?' He motioned down to his moving hat. 'I'm going to drop this in a minute.'

Danny rose to his feet, puzzled as to why his dad was wrestling with his hat. He approached cautiously. His dad had played tricks on him before. In fact, he was a lot like Sam in many ways.

'What is it, Dad?'

Danny's dad didn't get time to answer. Danny saw it. He knew what it was.

His heart skipped a beat when he caught sight of a tail flicking happily from under the hat. The secret was out. Danny's father flung his hat away like a magician revealing the wonder of a successful trick.

Under his arm, squirming and wriggling, was a small white pup. Danny ran to hold him.

The pup went crazy and so did Danny. 'Sam! Vicki!' he bellowed. 'Come out here, quick!'

Danny's father ruffled his son's hair. 'I had planned to get a sheep dog a while back, anyway,' he said. 'But since I don't need one any more, I thought it best to get a little dog.'

Danny was too excited to take much notice of what his dad had said. He was too busy laughing and fending off the little pup's boisterous affection. 'Ha, ha, keep still for a minute.'

Danny wrapped his fingers around the pup's middle, lifted it and held it at arm's length in front of his face. The tail never stopped. He was a soft ball of fluff with a pink belly. His nose was stubby and his bent ears flopped over his forehead. His tail curled cheekily onto his back. Danny put him down at his feet. The little pup didn't walk; he bounded around playfully, looking for a game. Then he saw Danny's shoelaces and lunged at them, taking them in his sharp little teeth and tugging. *Grrr.*

'Hey, get off!' Danny chuckled as he reached down and pulled him away.

'What do you want to call him?' his dad asked. 'What about Tippy the second?' he suggested.

Danny thought for a minute. Tippy was a good name, but there would never be another Tippy. As far as Danny was concerned there should be a statue of the little hero next to the soldier in front of the Mundowie Hall.

'No,' he answered. 'I couldn't call him Tippy.'

Sam and Vicki flew through the front door and off the verandah. They saw the pup, laughed and made a lot of noise. The little fellow seemed to like it. He yapped and spun about.

Sam and Vicki dropped to their knees. Sam set off on all fours and walked with the pup. 'What are we going to call him?' he asked.

At that moment the pup snapped a biscuit from Vicki's hand. 'Ow! You've got sharp teeth!' She was pouting as she looked at her dad and said, very loudly, 'He shouldn't snap like that.' She pointed at the puppy. 'You are a silly-billy,' she scolded.

'He is,' grinned Danny. 'Hey! That's it!' he said. 'Billy. Let's call him Billy.'

There were loud cheers of agreement. Vicki forgot about her biscuit. She smiled and clapped. 'I thought of it, didn't I, Danny? I was the one who thought of that name.'

'Billy it is then,' said their dad, pushing his hat from his forehead.

Danny looked at his dad. 'Where did you get him?'

'Mark Thompson saw an advertisement in the *Port Bilton Times*. He told his dad and his dad told me.'

'Mark Thompson?' said Danny.

Danny's dad nodded. 'Yeah, that's right. Mark misses Tippy too, you know. He loved him. His dad said that he'd never seen Mark cry as hard as he did the day he heard about Tippy and the snake.'

Danny was stunned. Mark Thompson had cried?

'He loved that little dog of yours, you know,' his dad continued. 'When you weren't here spoiling him he was over at the Thompsons'. Mark liked having him around. He used to feed him doughnuts and let him rest on his bed. He wanted a dog of his own, but his dad didn't want one once they sold the farm and thought they might move to the city.'

'But I didn't think Mark and his dad *were* moving to the city.'

'Well, they're not sure yet, he's got the truck, but who knows?'

Danny frowned. 'But Mr Thompson hates the city.'

'Hmm, I know.'

He gazed at his dad.

'Like you; you don't like the city much, do you, Dad?'

Danny's dad looked away. 'Not really,' he sighed. 'But I guess you get used to it.'

Danny nodded pensively. He wasn't sure he could.

Before Danny could drift into deeper thought, Billy took hold of his shoelace again.

Grrr.

Danny shook his leg. 'Get off, you little beast!' Billy let go and immediately skirted playfully around in preparation for another attack.

Before he could latch on again, Danny reached down and picked him up. 'Come on,' he said to Vicki and Sam. 'Let's take him over to show Mark.'

They headed off across the road with Billy's tail spinning in a blur.

Vicki danced to make her dress twirl and made up a song. 'Silly Billy, I love you. La, dee, da, dee, da, dee, dum. Silly Billy.'

Danny and Sam looked at Vicki, then each other, smirked and suddenly burst into a run.

'Hey!' Vicki cried, forgetting her song and flying from a skip to a run. 'Wait up!'

6
The Rope Bridge

Danny and Sam were pushing and pulling each other playfully in the passageway. Their stomping feet rumbled on the wooden floorboards. They weren't fighting; they were just being silly. Every time Danny came near, Sam pushed, bumped or swung Danny away. Of course, Danny always came back for more. It was great fun.

Spinning and bumping, tugging and swinging, he bounced from the walls of the passage like a silver ball in a pinball machine. He was laughing hard and couldn't stop. His body felt floppy and weak. He liked the feeling.

'Bump me again,' Danny chuckled. 'But not too hard.'

'No, I'll spin you this time,' Sam replied.

'Okay,' said Danny. 'Grab my shirt and spin me fast. Make me dizzy.'

Sam was keen. 'Right, you asked for it. Hang on.'

Sam took the tail of Danny's shirt in his hands and whizzed him around and around. Danny's outstretched arms thumped the walls. The boys laughed raucously.

Weak and floppy with laughter, Danny lost his balance and dropped to his knees with a dull thud.

Sam took hold of his brother's arm and dragged him along. 'Come on,' he said. 'Up you get. I'll spin you again.'

'Okay,' Danny laughed. 'Just wait until I get up.'

Sam pulled harder. Danny staggered to his feet.

The boys bumped into each other again and cried out happily, 'Whoa, ho, ho, ho.'

They were loud, but not as loud as their father when he suddenly stormed into the dull light at the end of the passageway. 'That's enough!' he roared viciously. He'd been in the kitchen sorting through folders and papers. 'Now get outside!'

Stunned, the boys stopped. Sam's eyes were sparkling. He smiled brightly up at his father. 'What did we do, Dad?' he asked innocently.

His dad took a step forward. He loomed in the darkest part of the passageway. His unshaven face was shadowed. 'Don't answer me back!' he snarled.

Sam's smile quickly faded.

Then pointing sharply to the back door, his dad yelled, 'I said get outside!'

Danny stared at his dad as he edged past and thought he looked different. Maybe it was just that he hadn't had a shave and wasn't wearing his hat and he looked tired. Or maybe it was the dull light of the passageway. He just didn't look right.

Danny was distracted from his thoughts by the sound of his mum's footsteps. She walked, soft and calm, into the passageway and put her hands gently on the boys' shoulders. 'Off you go,' she said quietly. 'Your dad's trying to think.'

Clutching at his forehead, Danny's dad slunk back into the kitchen. The boys walked behind him as quietly as a snake slithers through spring grass. Their dad slumped into a chair at the kitchen table. He had his back to them. Envelopes and papers surrounded his elbows. There were folders stacked at his feet in leaning towers. Danny's mum walked the boys to the back door and pushed it open. 'Vicki's down the back. She's dragging things out of the shed to make a cubbyhouse in the old pepper trees. She won't be able to do it alone. Why don't you go and help her?'

The boys walked out the back door and headed toward the shed.

Halfway down Danny broke the silence. 'What's wrong with Dad?' he asked.

Sam glanced back to the house and shrugged his shoulders. He hung his head and kicked up dust. 'I don't know,' he said distantly. 'Probably just a headache.'

He playfully nudged Danny to unbalance him. 'We *were* pretty rowdy,' he chuckled.

'Yeah,' giggled Danny. 'No one could think above that racket.'

Sam grabbed Danny's shirt, swung him mischievously and took off. Danny laughed and stumbled dizzily after him.

Down at the shed, Vicki emerged from the shadows. She had her arms wrapped around a long piece of wood and was dragging it along. Her flowery dress was filthy. She had a dark grubby mark across her cheek and her hair clips were loose. Her long fine hair, gently curled at the temples, fell across her face. She was singing as usual. *Tra, la, la, la, dee, dah.*

Danny shook his head. She always seemed to be singing the same song. His mum was the same. Once she had a song in her head she'd sing it over and over again for days. Then she'd go and buy the song and *play it* over and over again for weeks.

Vicki stopped when she saw the boys. She blew away the annoying strand of hair that hung over her eyes with a strong puff of air from her bottom lip.

Her face filled with delight. 'Hey boys,' she sparked. 'Do you want to help me?' Vicki dropped the piece of wood and skipped over to them. Her hair flapped at her shoulders. 'I've got this really good idea.'

She stood next to Danny and looked up into the branches of the big pepper trees. Her face was scrunched because the sun was in her eyes. Vicki pointed to the trees. 'I want to build a house up there with the birds.'

With a hand shielding his eyes, Danny gazed up into the sparks of sunlight flickering through the leaves of the tree. He squinted. 'Yeah, I think we can do that.'

He had no idea how, so he looked to his big brother. 'Can't we, Sam?'

Sam nodded. 'Yeah, we can do that.'

Vicki bounced on the spot and clapped loudly. 'Yaaayyy! I'll get more stuff from the shed.'

They all set to work.

Sam took charge. He was a good builder. His Lego constructions were incredible. There was a whole city on their bedroom floor once, with streets, houses, offices, institute halls and a freeway that went under his bed that he called the bed-tunnel freeway. When he finished constructing it he took some model aeroplanes he'd built and he and Danny flew about in dogfights above the Lego city. They dropped bombs made of marbles and cheered at the cracking sound of exploding Lego until the city lay in ruins. Then they rebuilt it and started again. It was wicked!

But some of the best things Sam created were made with junk – like the huge cardboard-box castle that sat under the window and the two tin-can tractors. These were made of a tin can with wheels, a little wooden seat and an engine drawn in feltpen on the side, and they sat on his bedside cupboard. They had a rubber band that ran through the centre of the can and somehow made them zoom along when it was wound up. Danny didn't understand how.

Two kites with bamboo frames and clear plastic

coverings hung on one wall. Sam had cut small round holes into the bamboo so that the kites would whistle like flutes when they flew. He'd read a book that said such kites were used in ancient wars and flown over armies at night to make ghostly sounds to scare the enemy. Sam loved the idea and put it into practice by terrifying Mark Thompson one windy night.

Danny loved it when Sam was inventing or building. It usually meant an exciting adventure would follow. Danny was amazed at the way Sam's mind worked and how he made little dreams come true. He was convinced that one day Sam would become someone very important – like an inventor, or scientist, or space explorer, or someone else who would be of enormous help to the world.

With great anticipation, Danny watched as Sam surveyed the site. He wandered thoughtfully, plans taking shape in his mind. Danny followed as Sam walked around the trees examining their trunks and branches. Then he strode into the tractor shed to check out what he could use in construction.

Danny's excitement was building. He couldn't wait to see how his brother was going to make Vicki's dream of a house in the trees with the birds come true. Danny wondered if it was going to be as grand as Sam's cardboard-box castle creation. If it was, Danny would not be surprised at all. A tree castle would be a fine thing to have.

Sam climbed the tree to look for the best building spot. Where the leaves were thickest he stood on a chunky branch that ran parallel with the ground. The branch forked off at a perfect point and spread like a giant hand holding a small jewel in its palm. 'We'll build the floor here,' Sam called, pointing to his feet. 'Across these two branches.' He stood astride the two thick prongs of the fork. 'It'll be perfect.' He looked across to the other pepper tree, which wasn't far away. 'We can build two houses,' he said. 'One in each tree and then . . . link them with a rope bridge.'

Vicki bounced up and down clapping her hands for the second time in only a few minutes. 'Yay! Yaaaaaay!'

Danny was excited, but resisted the urge to bounce. He could imagine two perfect tree houses with a rope bridge just like those that stretched across dangerous canyons in places like Argentina and Brazil. And it was going to be right here in his backyard. Brilliant! This was going to be a good day.

Vicki stopped bouncing and stood in front of Danny. She suddenly looked very serious. 'I get to choose the best house,' she declared loudly, with hands on hips. 'It was my idea. I get to choose.'

Danny put his hands on her shoulders. 'All right, all right. You get to choose.'

Danny and Vicki watched Sam climb down. 'Let's get started,' he said as he marched toward the tractor shed. Intensely curious, Danny and Vicki followed like sheep.

'How are we going to get everything up there, Sam?' Danny asked.

Sam waved a dismissive hand. 'Don't worry, I've got that all figured out,' he said.

Vicki quickened her step and skipped up beside Sam. 'Remember, I get to choose the best house,' she repeated.

'You'll have a hard choice,' Sam replied. 'They're both going to be pretty good.'

Vicki frowned thoughtfully. 'Will you help me choose then?'

'Of course,' Sam grinned shiftily. 'I'll choose for you if you like.'

Vicki was happy.

The patch of ground beneath the trees soon looked like a building site. There were old pieces of wood dumped in a small pile, bags, ropes, tins and wooden boxes. Sam clipped on a tool belt that held a hammer, some pliers and a pouch containing an assortment of nails. Vicki and Danny were in the shed pulling out more wood. Vicki was wearing huge leather gloves so that she didn't get splinters or spiders on her hands. Danny had found them for her after taking a tiny splinter from her thumb that was as fine as a strand of hair and hardly visible; it had sent her into a screaming frenzy.

Using strands of wire twisted and tied securely, Sam hung a pulley in the tree. He threaded a rope through it and let one end drop to the ground. It dangled like a snake. His idea was to tie anything heavy he might need to the rope at ground level, then haul it up into the tree – just like a crane on a skyscraper. Danny was in awe of his brother; he would never have thought of such a thing.

The first item they hoisted into the tree was an old wooden picket gate that their dad had made once. There were ten splintery pickets with small gaps. It looked rough, but it was strong. They had all tested its strength by bouncing on it in the shed; Vicki gave it a particularly long bouncing test. 'I'll use this for the floor,' Sam had suggested. 'It will look like the decking that some of those fancy houses have around their swimming pools.'

Sam waited in the tree as Danny and Vicki took the dangling rope and tied the gate with lots of ugly knots.

'Make sure you tie it on properly,' Sam called.

'Don't worry,' replied Danny, looking down at the intestine of knots they'd created. 'It's tied on all right.'

Sam slowly pulled the old gate, spinning and swaying, up into the branches. The pulley squeaked and Danny was reminded of images he'd seen on TV of huge cranes hauling girders to the top of city buildings under construction.

Sam peered down to see Danny and Vicki standing directly beneath the swinging gate.

'Hey! You idiots!' he yelled. 'Stand back in case it falls.' All good building sites should consider the safety of their workers.

'We tied lots of good knots,' Vicki called back.

'I don't care!' Sam snapped. 'Stand back because if it falls it'll kill you.'

The thought of dying under a killer gate dropped from the sky made Vicki walk away very quickly. She ended up standing all the way back near the house.

Danny watched Sam struggle. The gate wasn't heavy, but it was awkward. Sam couldn't pull it into the tree by himself. He nearly fell out trying.

'Come up and help me, Danny.'

Danny was happy to climb up and help.

Together, the boys quickly pulled it into position. They laid it across the forked branches and then tied it on with wire, small pieces of thin rope and a lot of nylon string. Sam checked all of Danny's knots and once it was secure they sat on it for the first time.

'This is brilliant!' Danny said, looking in all directions.

The boys could see into the shed below where the old tractor sat silent. They looked through the leaves past the house to the panoramic view of dusty Mundowie and beyond.

Danny was looking north to the gentle roll of endless hills and the patchwork of crooked fences. Sam was looking south to the big creek and the huge trees, their branches spattered with flocks of restless cockatoos.

Below them Vicki had moved to stand on a long piece of wood that Danny had placed on the top of the small pile of building materials. She was making it teeter like a seesaw. *Tra, la, la, la, dee, dah.*

Billy was chasing chickens and creating panic. Danny thought of Tippy and felt sad for only an instant because funny memories of Tippy pushed any sadness away. Danny smiled and fondly compared the chicken-chasing styles of the two dogs.

Tippy's style had been more aggressive. He loved to bare his teeth, act tough and strut to show the chickens he was boss. And when he was finished he would run to Danny to have his ears ruffled and get his approving pat. 'You little bully.'

Billy on the other hand was just silly. He didn't look as though he wanted to take charge and didn't seem interested in their food scraps either. Maybe that would come later as he grew, but for now he just liked to chase them. To him, chasing chickens was a game and he could play by himself, he didn't need anyone else – the chickens had no choice but to join in.

Danny watched the little dog run at them again. The chickens huddled together in panic.

Pertakeeeerk. Cluuuuuck. Cluck, cluck, cluck.

Yap! Yap! Yap! What a great game.

When Billy stopped yapping, Sam suddenly clutched Danny's arm. 'Look,' he said, pointing toward the sound of a car roaring along the dusty road that dipped into the creek. Danny saw only swirling dust at first. Then he saw the car growl up out of the creek and into the town. The boys knew who it was and suddenly understood why their dad had been wildly angry. It was the man from the bank. Danny's dad didn't seem to like him very much.

The boys tracked the car all the way to the front fence.

Vicki stopped singing. Billy left the chickens and ran to greet the visitor.

The car pulled up and the dust it created drifted across the house. Through the haze the boys saw a leg in dark trousers and black shiny shoes appear at the bottom of the car door as it opened. The man stood up and stiffened his shoulders, then took a bag from the back of his car and walked up the pathway toward the house.

His name was Adolf, or at least that's what Danny's dad called him. Danny couldn't understand why his dad didn't like Adolf.

It was true, his black hair *was* a bit greasy and he didn't like getting dust on his shoes, always giving his toes a little polish on the leg of his trousers just before he walked to the front door, but he seemed like a nice man. He'd visited a lot in recent weeks and had given Danny, Sam and Vicki each a great moneybox. They were metal and modelled on the bank building in the city. Danny had hidden his under his bed behind his sleeping bag, basketball and boogie board. He was saving and already had seventeen dollars and fifty-five cents.

Adolf walked through the front yard. He shook a leg at Billy, who barked at his heels. The boys lost sight of him when he walked up the front steps and under the verandah.

'I hope he doesn't keep Dad talking all day,' said Danny. 'He'll be even grumpier if he does.'

'Forget all that,' said Sam. 'Let's keep working.'

'What do you want to do next?' asked Danny.

Sam's eyes lit up. 'Let's start the rope bridge.'

'Yeah!' Danny exclaimed. He leant over and peered down at Vicki. 'We need a rope, Vicki.'

Vicki didn't stop swaying on her little seesaw. 'Why don't you come and get one yourself.'

'You won't get first choice of the houses if you don't help.'

Vicki stopped immediately. She looked up at Danny's face peering down at her through the leaves and adjusted her giant gloves. 'Yes I will!' she said as she marched off to hunt for a rope. 'Sam said.'

The boys climbed out of the tree and Sam set about

designing his bridge. He knew how the rope bridge should look, but just to be sure he had it clear in his mind, he drew a picture on a piece of white wood with one of his dad's carpenter's pencils.

Danny and Vicki watched over his shoulder.

'I wish I could draw like that,' said Danny, thinking aloud.

'Can we build it now?' asked Vicki, picking up a piece of timber.

'Put that down,' said Sam. 'I'll do it.'

'But I have to help.' Vicki pouted. 'Or you won't let me choose the best house.'

'Will you shut up about the best house,' said Sam, sorting through the timber. 'You can have it, all right?'

Sam set to work. The pieces of wood he chose were the perfect size. Most of them were from a crate they broke apart with mad hammering. He laid them out on the ground so they looked just like a bridge. He wanted to be sure he had enough slats so that the gaps between them weren't too wide. They all walked across it to test it.

Danny and Vicki held the wood while Sam drilled. He was the only one allowed to use the drill. Their dad had showed him how and had even stuck a little 'L' for 'Learner' on the top.

Sam made two holes at the end of each slat through which rope could be threaded and tied.

Vicki didn't understand rope bridge construction. 'Why are we drilling holes?' she asked.

'So we can thread rope through them, like threading beads,' Sam answered.

'Why?'

'Because the slats . . .'

'Slats? What are they?'

'The pieces of wood you will walk on when you cross the bridge.'

'Oh, them.'

'Yes, they have to be all linked together otherwise when we hang it between the two trees it will all fall apart.'

Vicki still didn't really understand, but she didn't think she should ask another question. Sam was sounding grumpy.

'Oh right,' she nodded unconvincingly.

Sam made four holes in each slat, two at each end. There was a lot of drilling, but despite the noise their parents didn't come outside. Occasionally, Danny spied his mum at the kitchen window. Vicki waved every time she saw her.

Once the holes were drilled Vicki was put in charge of threading rope through them. She was good at threading beads, so she thought she would be good at threading rope. She had a lot of trouble with the splinters and pushing the fat rope through the holes though. The boys knew she was never going to finish it alone, but that didn't matter. It kept her busy and out of their way while they finished constructing both tree houses.

Neither of the cubbies they built had walls. Both were basically just a platform in a tree. They didn't really need walls. The leaves of the trees were thick enough curtains to hide them away. They hung hessian bags as a roof on the second house.

Vicki chose that one. She liked the roof. It was also the lower of the two and Sam convinced her that it was better not to be too high off the ground. He told her about falling and splitting her head open. Vicki had an image of her head exploding like a watermelon dropped from a great height – that's how Sam had described the impact.

'Oooh.' She crinkled her nose in repulsion. 'I could lose my brain.'

It was exciting to sit up in the cubbies. But by far the best part of the construction was the rope bridge. It was the middle of the afternoon when Sam finally finished the threading Vicki had started and secured the wooden slats with the knots he'd learnt in Scouts.

'Now all we have to do,' said Sam, scratching his head, 'is to get it up into the tree.'

'We can use the pulley to tug one end up, tie it on

and then do the same with the other end, can't we?' said Danny.

Sam patted him on the back. 'Yeah.' He grinned. 'I suppose we can.'

And that's what they did.

Hanging the bridge was awkward. Vicki stayed on the ground shouting useless instructions. 'Up a bit . . . no over a bit . . . too far . . . it's hanging too low, pull it up!'

The rope bridge, swinging with each tug of the pulley rope, was a wonderful sight as it rose slowly into the treetops. At first, when Sam had only secured one end, it hung like a huge rope ladder.

Danny helped pull the second side into place and had to use all his strength to stop it from falling while Sam tied it to the tree.

At first it looked crooked and unsafe.

Vicki didn't like it. 'I'm not walking across that,' she said.

'It's not finished yet!' snapped Sam. 'It's not tied on properly and I have to get the tension right.'

'Tension? What's tension?'

Sam shook his head, mumbled something and turned away without answering. He began adjusting ropes and knots.

He spent a long time securing both sides. He checked and double-checked his knots. The ropes he added for holding on and keeping balance ran either side of the bridge at about hip height and looked a bit floppy, but overall it looked just as Danny had imagined it would.

Standing in the tree and looking across the bridge for the first time was exciting. Danny caught hold and made it sway a little.

The bridge wasn't very long. There were only nine steps and each of them was evenly spaced. Sam had used his foot to measure the spaces.

When Sam finally tied the last rope to a branch using four fat knots in a bunch like a fist everyone was ready to walk across.

Vicki sat in her house and looked across at her brothers. She took hold of the rope bridge and swung it gently. She glanced down to the ground and felt dizzy. 'Who's going first?' she called.

Billy was sitting beneath them looking up and tilting his head curiously.

Yap! Yap!

Vicki lay on her stomach and waved down to him. 'Hey Billy boy,' she sang.

Billy wagged his tail and then sat waiting.

So did Danny. 'You should go first, Sam,' he said. 'You built it.'

Sam nodded. 'Yeah, all right.'

He grasped the rope and tugged at it. 'Feels good I reckon.'

He took his first tentative step. The bridge swayed.

'Jeez! Careful!' said Danny, grabbing at the bridge. 'Try to keep it still.'

Sam bent his knees. 'I am trying! Now will you shut up?'

Vicki watched with wide eyes. So did Danny and Billy.

Sam was concentrating. It was hard to keep the bridge steady. Everything swayed, no matter how hard Sam tried to keep it still.

He was on the fourth step when Billy barked and startled him. Sam jumped. The bridge swayed. Sam clung to the floppy side ropes, but they swung away from him. His arms were stretched wide apart. Despite his best attempts not to slip, using a lot of hip gyration and foot shuffling, he lost his balance. One leg was suddenly hanging below the bridge while the other was hooked around one of the steps. He was still clinging to the side rope. But only just.

'Hang on, Sam!' Vicki cried. 'Don't fall. Don't fall. Your head will open up and you'll lose your brain!'

'Shut up!'

Danny took a step onto the bridge, which made it swing more. Sam yelled at him. 'Get off! You're making it worse.'

'I was coming to help.'

'Well don't! I'm all right.'

Danny stepped back and looked on, feeling useless. It was like watching a movie, a really good movie that kept you on the edge of your seat.

Vicki and Danny were watching so intently and Sam was hanging so precariously that not one of them noticed Adolf slink into his car and drive away.

Sam scrambled and kicked. He pulled and grappled determinedly. And, like all good heroes in movies, he regained his balance and stood once more. He made the crossing. Once at Vicki's house he lifted his hands triumphantly above his head.

Vicki clapped.

Danny gave a cheer. 'I'll give it a try now, shall I?' he called.

Sam looked to the bridge. He took hold and shook it. 'No, no, you'd better not. We need to stop it from wobbling so much first. You'll fall off if we don't.'

Danny glanced at the ground. 'Okay,' he said. He was disappointed, but didn't want to split his head open. They all climbed down.

As soon as the children had gathered together beneath the two pepper trees to make plans to steady the bridge, their mother called to them. 'Come inside, children, please. Hurry up.'

They hurried inside, Vicki skipping, Danny jogging and Sam walking, all expecting cake or biscuits or . . . but their mother didn't look at them. She was looking out of the back window.

Danny thought she must be coming down with a cold. She was sniffing and had a handkerchief in her hand. Danny's dad was nowhere to be seen. Before their mother could say anything the tractor roared to life and the boys leapt to their feet. 'Hey wait up, Mum!' they cried. 'Dad's going on the tractor. We want to go with him.'

'Me too!' said Vicki.

'No!' said their mother firmly.

'But where's he going?' asked Sam.

'He's going to finish fixing that fence by the creek and wants to do it alone, so sit down.'

She still didn't turn around, but the children sat.

'But he might need us,' said Danny.

His mum's shoulders lifted as she drew in a big strong breath. Then she said with a sigh, 'Yes, he does need you, but not at the creek. He needs you here to pack things away.'

'To pack what away?' asked Danny.

'Everything we have,' said Danny's mum. She took a long, deep breath. 'We're leaving the farm, children.' She breathed again. 'We're moving away from Mundowie.'

Silence.

◆

Danny's dad returned after dark as the children were eating their dinner.

He walked into the kitchen. All heads turned to look at him. He took his hat off (the one with the oil stain that looked like a tiny map of Africa) and placed it on a chair.

Danny didn't like the silence.

'Did you fix the fence, Dad?' he asked.

'Yep, all done.'

'So the sheep won't try to fly,' said Vicki with concern. 'They won't squish?'

Danny's dad had no idea what she was talking about. 'Fly?' he said, puzzled. 'No, the sheep won't fly.'

'Good,' Vicki said.

Danny threw glances back and forth between his mum and dad. He was about to say something, but Sam beat him to it.

Luckily, Sam said what Danny was thinking. 'So what are we going to do?'

Danny's dad sat at the table and looked at each of the children in turn. Danny saw a turtle-like tiredness in his eyes.

'Well, we're moving to the city,' he announced. 'I was a carpenter once, so I guess I can be a carpenter again.'

'The city!' cried Sam. 'Wicked!'

Danny felt his stomach turn upside down. 'Couldn't we just live here and not have the farm, like Mark Thompson's dad?'

'No, I'm sorry, Danny, there's no work for me here.'

Danny tilted his head curiously. 'Why did you fix the fence, Dad, if we're not staying?'

Danny's dad took him by the shoulders and gently squeezed. 'I don't want anyone coming onto the farm and saying I didn't look after the place.'

Danny straightened himself. 'No one would say that, Dad,' he said, taking offence at the thought. 'You're a good farmer. It's not your fault the sky didn't rain at the right time.'

Danny's dad managed a smile. 'Well, when you put

it like that,' he said, gently ruffling Danny's hair, 'I suppose not, Danny.'

Danny's mum and dad embraced. Danny's mum buried her face in his shoulder and dusty shirt.

Danny got up and went to his room; he never knew what to do when grown-ups cried.

In bed Danny and Sam lay awake.

'I knew this was coming,' said Sam quietly.

'How did you know?' asked Danny.

'Come off it, Danny. Don't you notice anything?'

'Like what?'

'The bank meetings, the papers all over the table, Dad's extra job fixing the playground. He always said he needed a sheep dog, but he didn't get one when Tippy died; he got a dog he knew would be okay in a city house.'

Danny suddenly had a rude awakening. Sam was right. Danny thought back. When they were painting the playground his dad had said something about trying to hang on. And when Billy came he *had* said something about not needing a sheep dog. There were other things as well, but Danny hadn't noticed because he'd been too busy with the adventures of each day. There didn't seem to be any need to think about tomorrow. It was always too far away.

Sam rolled over. 'Anyway, the city will be brilliant, there's heaps to do.'

'There's heaps to do here,' said Danny.

'Yeah, but not like the city.'

Danny put his hands behind his head and stared up at the ceiling.

'No,' he mumbled.

As tired as he was, Danny couldn't sleep. He tossed and turned. When Sam started snoring he crawled out of bed and went diving into the darkness under his bed in search of his moneybox. When he found it he waddled off toward the kitchen. Billy jumped from the end of the bed and wandered with him, hoping for food.

Bright moonlight streamed through the kitchen window. Danny peered out. The world was silver. The brilliant moon, not quite full, sat like a huge pearl on a bed of black velvet surrounded by millions of tiny diamonds. Danny felt as though he was gazing through the window of a dream. The dark didn't matter.

Danny sat at the table. The clock was ticking and the fridge humming. He opened the little cap at the bottom of his moneybox. Billy looked on, licking his lips. Danny emptied all the money out onto the tablecloth and counted – it was seventeen dollars and fifty-five cents. Danny piled all the notes and coins neatly and left the money next to the folder that said *BANK* on the spine.

He gazed dreamily out of the kitchen window

down to the shed. The rope bridge reached out to him from the deepest darkness beneath the shelter of the pepper trees and into the moonlight. He had to climb it, just once. He had no idea when they were actually leaving, but if they left the next day he would never get the chance to do it.

Danny Allen walked out into the night with Billy by his side. The yard was wonderful in moonlight. Everything was so still and so peaceful. There was nothing to be afraid of.

Danny walked down toward the shed, conscious of the sound of his own footsteps. Unfamiliar in the shadows, the old tractor was like a sleeping monster. Danny climbed the tree, slowly but surely. His boots flipped and flopped without socks. Beneath the tree the ground was decorated with puzzle-like pieces of moonlight shadow. Billy walked through them, sniffing, wondering where the chickens were.

Danny climbed to sit on the cubby house. Under the leaves it was very dark. He stood to grasp the rope bridge.

He held the side ropes. They were still loose. The bridge never looked very high, but once he was standing on it the ground seemed miles away.

Danny didn't think about falling, or his head splitting apart like a dropped watermelon. He took a deep breath and stood tall, then took his first step alone, out into darkness. Ahead, only two steps away, was the brilliance of the moonlight.

Like a moth, Danny headed for the light. The bridge swayed with each cautious step.

Before Danny knew it, he was halfway across. He smiled to himself. This wasn't hard. He wasn't going to get hurt. He wouldn't fall now. His head wouldn't

crack apart and spill his brains on the dust by the tractor shed. There was nothing to be afraid of, or worried about.

Danny stopped in the full glow of the moonlight. He stood in the middle of the rope bridge. He looked across the roof of the house to the Mundowie Institute Hall. The moonlight made the white marble soldier statue glow like the ghost gums down at the creek.

Danny sniffed the air like Billy. He looked in all directions at everything he could see. The moonlight on the roof and the white chimney; the silhouette of the rooftops across the road; Mark Thompson's rooftop.

Even the white gravel road that cut through the town was glowing. It didn't look hard and full of stones. It looked like a fluffy blanket. Danny didn't want to get off the bridge. He lay down on his back as if it were a hammock. He kept a firm grip on the ropes and stared up at the stars.

This was a magical world.

This was Danny Allen's place.

7
Leaving

The day Danny Allen left Mundowie his house was a whirlwind of activity. Mark Thompson's dad had offered his truck to help with the move. He was carting furniture out the front door with Danny's dad.

'Watch your step, don't fall backwards.'

'Hang on, my fingers are trapped. A little to the left, hold it! Hold it!'

In the yard Billy was playing his scatter-the-chickens game.

Yap! Yap!

Pertakeerk, cluck, cluck, cluck.

Danny's mum was directing everyone. Clumps and strands of her hastily clipped hair were hanging untidily. She stood in the kitchen doorway pointing and barking orders.

'Danny, pick up that last box in the bedroom and help Sam take it out to the truck. Vicki, stop dancing and help, please.'

'In a minute,' Vicki replied as she readied herself for a twirl across the open kitchen floor. She loved the empty house. The bare floorboards and empty rooms provided her with stage after stage upon which to spin and spring about.

Danny didn't like the emptiness. 'Stop fooling around,' he grumbled, deliberately walking into Vicki's twirling path. 'You have to help.'

Vicki stopped and frowned at him. 'Get out of the way. I will in a minute.'

Before Danny could argue, Sam called to him from the passageway. 'Danny, hurry up!'

Vicki put her hands to her hips, tapped her foot impatiently, waited for Danny to get out of her way, and then went on twirling.

At the front of the house the old Thompson truck was loaded with cupboards, beds, the fridge, boxes and suitcases. At the very top of the furniture mountain sat the old kennel that Billy had inherited from Tippy.

Not everything would fit on the truck. Some of the furniture had been stored in the Wallaces' shed. Aunty Jean thought it was a good idea. 'It means you'll have to come back to visit,' she said with a laugh.

When the house was completely empty Danny didn't like wandering through it. The echo was weird and Vicki's non-stop dancing annoyed him.

Once the chickens had been rounded up and caged, the deserted yard was eerily quiet. And looking down toward the tractor shed to see the rope bridge hanging alone made Danny's stomach churn.

Danny's mum said, 'I hope we've got everything. I'd hate to leave anything behind.'

'Oh no!' Danny suddenly cried. 'I *have* forgotten something. Don't go yet. Don't go.'

With that he took off across the road. Billy took off after him. *Yap! Yap!* He gave up the chase when he realised he was going to be left behind.

Everyone was puzzled, even Billy, as they watched Danny run off.

'He's not running away again, is he?' said Sam. 'I can't wait to get to the city and I want to get there before it's dark.'

Vicki didn't like the sound of the city in the dark.

She swallowed and said, 'We *will* get there before it's dark, won't we, Mum?'

'Not at this rate.'

Sam nudged Vicki. 'It doesn't matter,' he said. 'The city is brilliant at night. All the lights look like the stars have fallen from the sky.'

Vicki looked up at Sam. 'Will it be good in the city?'

'You've been there,' said Sam. 'Remember all the shops we went to?'

'Yeah,' Vicki nodded.

'We'll be able to go every day if we want.'

Vicki liked the shops. She had bought her favourite necklace there the last time they went. But then she looked at Sam, tilting her head quizzically to one side, and said, 'But where will we get tadpoles?'

Sam shook his head. 'I give up. You're hopeless.'

Vicki didn't understand his terse reaction. She thought it was a fair question.

Danny ran across the road and under his lookout tree, past the Mundowie Institute Hall without a salute to the white soldier statue standing guard and off toward the creek. As he flew past the playground he heard a voice calling to him. 'Danny! Danny Allen. Hey there!'

It was Aunty Jean Wallace. Danny didn't stop.

He waved to her as he passed. 'I'll be back in a minute, Aunty Jean.'

Down toward the creek he ran, racing through shadows, leaping dead logs, stomping with determined footsteps on the crackle-dry grass.

He flew away, leaping down a slope, arms waving like the wild flapping wings of the noisy cockatoos shrieking from the gum trees overhead.

Aunty Jean leant on her fence and smiled as she watched Danny race over a crest, then dip and disappear below a horizon of thick yellow weeds.

At the creek, Danny ran along its banks. As he passed each familiar landmark, he remembered different adventures. First there was the sheep track that they had slid down to go sand-dune surfing, then the drums that they made into a grandstand before they were the sad site of Tippy's death. Above the drums the lonely tyre hung over the dry creek bed and finally he passed the slope down which the tractor tube flew on muddy days. There were so many things to remember.

Danny didn't stop to reminisce; there wasn't time. He kept running until he reached the spot. His secret place.

Puffing hard he dropped to his knees. In he scrambled without fear. After all, the leaping vampire snake was dead now; Tippy had seen to that.

His eyes blinked furiously and fingers of dusty

sunlight reached into the darkness. Danny knelt and looked down at his treasures. The tadpole-hunting tin, full of little bits and pieces, sat next to the ram's skull. Danny scooped everything up and took one last look at his secret place, goosebumps pricking across his shoulders at the memory of his snake encounter. With the tin in his hand and the skull under his arm he scrambled from the half-darkness back into the light. Careful not to drop the tin or the skull he headed back to Mundowie.

Danny jogged up the slope and emerged from the shadows of the creek, and he spied Aunty Jean still at the fence.

Danny hurried over to her.

'Sorry, Aunty Jean,' he puffed. 'I had to get my things.'

Aunty Jean looked at the skull and the tin with a wry smile. She said, 'I've got something else for you. Can you carry one more thing?'

'What is it?' asked Danny.

She offered him a parcel wrapped in red crinkled wrapping paper which was obviously second-hand. 'This is for you,' she said, tucking it under his arm.

Danny looked at the present. 'Thanks, Aunty Jean. What is it?'

'It's a surprise,' she said with a wink. 'But don't open it until later. Perhaps when you're driving along.'

Aunty Jean reached out and cuddled Danny, sheep skull and all, and gave him a peck on the cheek. 'Good luck, Danny Allen.' Her voice was crackly like a radio not quite tuned in to the station. 'We'll see you when you come back to visit. And don't worry; we'll take good care of your furniture.'

'And Mundowie,' added Danny.

Aunty Jean ruffled Danny's hair. 'Oh yes,' she chuckled. 'Of course.'

'Thank you, Aunty Jean,' Danny said.

Danny turned away and set off to say goodbye to his empty home.

◆

When Danny arrived back everyone was standing in front of the truck. His mum looked at his load, shook her head and said, 'So have you got everything you need now, Danny?'

Danny looked at his mum and dad, at Sam and Vicki, who had Billy in her arms, at his tin, the skull and the red box being crushed under his arm. After a thoughtful pause he nodded firmly. 'Yep, I have . . . I think.'

Sam and Vicki were going in the car with Billy. Danny wasn't going in the car. He'd won the right, after a hotly contested tournament of paper, scissors, rock, for the first ride in the truck.

He sat between his dad and Mr Thompson.

Danny looked out the window when he heard Mark Thompson calling from across the road.

'Hey boys! Yo!'

Danny leant forward to peer past his dad. Mark was at the side of the Mundowie Institute Hall.

The Thompsons were staying in Mundowie for the time being.

'Hey Danny!' Mark yelled. 'Remember the ten.'

Danny beamed. He leant across his dad and stuck his head out the window. 'Yeah!'

'Watch this,' Mark called. 'Watch.'

Danny gazed out of the open window with his eyes peeled on Mark.

Mark Thompson spun round, took his footy from under his arm and kicked it at the Mundowie Hall. Danny watched, expecting to see it sail over the top, but it didn't. In fact, it didn't even go close. It hit the gutter and bounced back.

Mark jumped and caught the ball in his hands. He tucked it under his arm. 'One day I'll get it over,' he called.

Danny shook his head. 'What do you mean?'

'I've never done it, Danny Allen.' He laughed. 'Never!'

Danny was shocked. 'What?'

With a crunch of gears, the truck slowly drew away from the house. Danny looked back and watched Mark try again and again to kick the ball over the Mundowie Hall. He couldn't even get it onto the roof. Danny watched Mark until he was lost in the dust.

Then Danny sat silent in the truck and looked to his dad. He wasn't wearing his farming hat, the one with the oil stain that looked like a tiny map of Africa.

Danny's dad looked down at the big tin with the wire handle that was sitting in Danny's lap.

'Why are you holding onto that, Danny?' he asked.

Danny lifted the tin. 'This is the tin we used for tadpole hunting.'

'Tadpole hunting?'

'Yeah.'

'Where? Not at the dam?'

'Yeah.'

'Your mum didn't tell me about that. And I thought I had made it perfectly clear that you weren't . . .' He stopped in mid sentence and sighed. 'Ah, what does it matter now? And anyway, I bet I don't know half the things you kids get up to.'

Danny smiled at his dad and thought about what he'd said. Then Danny thought back to his dad's bank visits, the bad seasons on the farm and the evenings his dad sat poring over the financial folders obviously in desperate trouble, but he didn't let on. And Danny thought, *Well, I don't know half the things you get up to either, Dad.*

Danny's dad leant over and peered into the tin. 'What have you got in there now? I know there aren't any tadpoles.'

Danny took things out one by one, starting with Tippy's collar. Danny held the collar and shook it gently to make it jingle.

Then he held up his baked head that his mum had cooked for him. Danny didn't need to explain that one, his dad knew all about it. He had varnished it to keep it preserved.

At the bottom of the tin were flaky remnants of the

snakeskin he'd found in rocks near the old Miller homestead the day Sam had surfed the Everest Dune. Danny didn't lift them as they would have dissolved in his fingers.

When he held up the tuft of wool belonging to Stanley the ram Danny told his dad the story of Mark Thompson, Sam and the ram race to the playground.

His dad laughed.

Danny went on to show some teeth from his ram's skull. He wasn't allowed to keep the whole skull so he had broken some teeth off and put them in.

When Danny finished showing his treasures, his dad patted his knee firmly. 'That's a great tin, son. Don't lose it, will you?'

Danny shook his head firmly. 'I won't ever, Dad.' Then he bent over and reached down to his feet. He held up the red box that Aunty Jean had given him. When he tore it open he was happy with what he found.

He offered the box to his dad. 'Aunty Jean's Anzac biscuit, Dad?'

'Wow! Cheers, mate.'

Mr Thompson took two.

The truck gathered speed and rumbled quickly along. Into the shadows of the creek it roared and rattled up the other side.

Danny munched on his biscuits and stared out of

the window wondering what tomorrow would bring. A song came on the radio. It was the Beatles' *Let It Be*. Danny's dad suddenly burst into song, like Danny's mother in the kitchen.

Danny was surprised by his dad's jocularity. Mr Thompson joined in and despite the sadly out of tune singing, Danny enjoyed the performance. Not wanting to be left out, he tried to whistle along – Mark Thompson had taught him how to whistle ages ago.

Whistling as badly as his dad was singing, Danny clung to his tin and looked to the road ahead. The truck, and everything in it, bounced in rhythm.

Danny Allen was city bound.